Finding
Cinderella

Also by Colleen Hoover

Finding Cinderella

A Novella

Colleen Hoover

ATRIA PAPERBACK

NEW YORK   LONDON   TORONTO   SYDNEY   NEW DELHI

ATRIA PAPERBACK

Atria Paperback
A Division of Simon & Schuster, Inc.
1230 Avenue of the Americas
New York, NY 10020

First Atria Paperback edition March 2014

ATRIA Paperback and colophon are trademarks of Simon & Schuster, Inc.

The Simon & Schuster Speakers Bureau can bring authors to your live event. For more information or to book an event, contact the Simon & Schuster Speakers Bureau at 1-866-248-3049 or visit our website at www.simonspeakers.com.

Cover design by Sarah Hansen
Cover photograph © Image Source/Getty Images

Manufactured in the United States of America

30   29   28   27   26   25   24   23   22   21

ISBN 978-1-4767-8328-4
ISBN 978-1-4767-7143-4

For Stephanie and Craig.
Fist bump.

A Note to My CoHorts

So many amazing things have happened over the past two years, and it's all thanks to each and every one of my readers. I originally released *Finding Cinderella* online for free as a thank-you to everyone who has made my life what it is today.

Never did I expect the reaction *Finding Cinderella* received. The feedback was one thing, but the fact that you all rallied together and begged for it in print was something I never expected. Here you all were with a free ebook in your hands. You had already read it, yet you still wanted it in paperback to grace your shelves. That is the highest compliment an author can receive, knowing her words mean that much to her readers.

After months of pleas, I have never been more excited for the release of a book than I am for this one. Because this one isn't on shelves because of me. It's on shelves because of *you*.

I dedicate this book to all of the awesomely insane CoHorts for their endless, unmatched support. I love you all!

My Cinderella Story

Two years ago I was living in a mobile home with my husband and three sons, and working at a job that paid $9 per hour. I was happy with what I had been given, but it was not exactly the life I had envisioned for my family or myself.

Since childhood, I dreamed of being a writer, but for thirty-one years I made excuse after excuse as to why I couldn't be one:

> *"I have no spare time."*
> *"My writing isn't good enough."*
> *"I'll never get published."*
> *"I'm too busy writing excuses to write a novel."*

In reality, the only reason I was not pursuing my dream was because I thought dreams were just that . . . *dreams*. Intangible. Unrealistic. Childish.

I've always been a realist, never looking at the glass half empty *or* half full. I'm the type of person who is just thankful to have a glass at *all*. That was exactly how I viewed my life two years ago. I never allowed myself to be ungrateful or wish for more.

My husband and I both come from low-income families, and we did our best to make ends meet and put ourselves through college. I took out student loans and we both worked full-time, trading days off so we didn't have to pay for child care. I received a Bachelor of Social Work from Texas A&M University–Commerce in December 2005, two months before giving birth to our third child.

After a few years of our moving around from rent-house to rent-house and my working as a social worker, my parents helped us buy a three-bedroom, two-bath singlewide mobile home that was barely more than one thousand square feet. I felt blessed to have three healthy children, a wonderful, supportive husband, and a roof over our heads.

As happy as I was, I felt like something was missing. That childhood dream of writing a book kept resurfacing and I kept pushing it back down with more excuses.

Then in October 2011, after watching one of my own children follow one of his dreams, I began to entertain the thought that maybe dreams *are* tangible.

My middle child, who was eight years old at the time, wanted to audition for the local community theater. I was thrilled at his bravery, but when he actually got the part, I was forced to face reality. There was no way I could work eleven-hour days and take him to rehearsals five evenings a week. My husband was working as a long-haul truck driver at the time and was home only a few days each month, so I was essentially a single mother. However, my children's happiness has always been my priority, and I was not about to let my son down. I received help from a friend who dropped him off at my work after school so we could make it to his rehearsals, while my mother watched my other two children.

For the next two months, I sat in the audience for three hours each evening watching rehearsals. I watched my son on stage and was filled with pride at seeing him pursue his passion at such a young age. Those moments prompted me to think about my own childhood passions and how much I dreamed of becoming a writer. When I was younger, I wrote during every free moment and on any surface I could find. My mother would enthusiastically read my "Mystery Bob" stories that I penned from crayon on scraps of paper stapled together. I continued to write for fun throughout high school and even pursued journalism my first year in college. However, after I married my high school sweetheart and had our first son by the age of twenty, my childhood dream began to fade as the responsibilities of real life set in. As much as I wanted to be a writer, it seemed impossible. Instead, I held on to my self-doubt and insecurities for ten years, allowing responsibility after responsibility to become my crutch.

As I sat in the audience of my son's rehearsals, I saw something in him that had long been dormant in myself—*creative passion.*

While it was a remarkable moment to see my son pursuing his dream, it was also a rude awakening. I was doing my children a disservice by setting the example that it's okay to put yourself last . . . to put your own desires on the back burner while you take care of everyone else. I made a promise to myself that night that I would start writing again, even if it was only for my own enjoyment. After coming to this realization, I began to find inspiration and motivation from other areas.

One of my biggest motivators came from an Avett Brothers concert I attended with my sister. It was one of the best experiences of my life, not because we were in the front row, but because of a few powerful seconds during their song "Head Full of Doubt, Road Full of Promise." I had heard these lyrics sung many times before, yet the meaning had never resonated with me until that very moment.

"Decide what to be, and go be it."

The sentence was simple and straightforward; yet it left a profound impression on me. For days, the words continued to repeat in my head until they finally sunk in: if I wanted to be a writer, there was no reason I couldn't *"go be it."* I pulled out my laptop at one of the play rehearsals, and I wrote the very first line to *Slammed*:

"Kel and I load the last two boxes into the U-Haul."

It was the first sentence to the book that would change my life.

At the time, I was writing the book only for myself, but my mother was a huge supporter of my writing. After all, she still had the riveting "Mystery Bob" stories I'd written in crayon. Even though I knew her opinion would be biased, I let her read what I had completed. She loved it, as any good mother would, and began pestering me for the next chapters.

I also allowed my boss and both of my sisters to read the first several chapters and they, too, asked for more. The fact that they wanted more of the story gave me the inspiration to continue. I enjoyed it so much that I wrote at every opportunity. I would put my children to bed at night, write until well after midnight and then have to be at work at seven o'clock the next morning. By the end of December, I had traded so much sleep in favor of writing that I had a complete manuscript. I also had three children who were now very adept at working a microwave.

When I reached those two final words, *The End*, I felt like I had just achieved my childhood dream, despite not having a real book, a publisher, or even an audience.

After word spread that I had written a book, friends and family began requesting to read it. I couldn't afford to have paperbacks printed, so I researched and found Amazon's Kindle Direct Publishing program. After days of more research and attempting to learn everything I could about self-publishing, I uploaded my book to Amazon.

I had no expectations. I never even tried to get the book traditionally published, because in my mind I had already achieved my dream of writing the book. I didn't think there was a chance that people who didn't know me would ever read it.

The opposite happened. Hundreds of people, complete strangers, started to order my book. I began receiving requests for a sequel from those readers and, since I enjoyed writing the first book so much, I was more than thrilled to deliver a sequel. I released *Point of Retreat* in February 2012. Soon after, I began receiving royalty payments. Everything was happening so fast, I held on to every moment, afraid it would all end overnight. Since the sales weren't guaranteed, I refused to accept the possibility that things could improve from there. I was waiting for the excitement, positive reviews, and requests for more books to come to an end, because it was all too good to be true.

But it didn't end. Every day brought new readers until the books eventually hit the *New York Times* Best Sellers List. Publishers took notice of the rapid success of both books and, after signing up with a literary agent, I accepted a publishing offer from Atria Books.

My life became so busy that I had to quit my job in order to focus on writing full-time. I was worried there wouldn't be enough money in it to support my family, but with the release of my third book, *Hopeless*, in December 2012, I was finally convinced that this was now my career. *Hopeless* went on to hit #1 on the *New York Times* Best Sellers List and was Amazon's best selling self-published e-book of 2013, and their sixteenth bestselling e-book overall of 2013.

We moved out of our mobile home less than ten months ago and now live in a lake house that we never thought could be ours. Each morning I wake up and I'm consumed with disbelief that this is now our life. We've been able to pay off all our debt and create college funds for our boys. We've also donated to several charities as a way to give back for all the incredible things that have happened to us.

In the past two years, I have gone from a mother who refused to believe that a childhood fantasy could become a reality, to a writer with five books that have all become *New York Times* Best Sellers, a free novella, and two more novels to be published this year.

Each of those books is tangible proof that if you have the courage to make them happen, dreams are very real and attainable. All you have to do is find what inspires you, which can be something as simple as a song lyric or a child's smile on stage. Then you have to make the long, brave effort, which can be as daunting as sitting down at a computer, facing a blank page, and not giving up until you reach the finish line.

Despite all the great experiences and accomplishments that have come after it, I still consider my proudest moment to be the first time I typed the words *The End.*

For that was my beginning.

Colleen Hoover

Finding
Cinderella

Prologue

"You got a tattoo?"

It's the third time I've asked Holder the same question, but I just don't believe it. It's out of character for him. Especially since I'm not the one who encouraged it.

"Jesus, Daniel," he groans on the other end of the line. "Stop. And stop asking me why."

"It's just a weird thing to tattoo on yourself. *Hopeless*. It's a very depressing term. But still, I'm impressed."

"I gotta go. I'll call you later this week."

I sigh into the phone. "God, this sucks, man. The only good thing about this entire school since you moved is fifth period."

"What's fifth period?" Holder asks.

"Nothing. They forgot to assign me a class, so I hide out in this maintenance closet every day for an hour."

Holder laughs. I realize as I'm listening to it that it's the first time I've heard him laugh since Les died two months ago. Maybe moving to Austin will actually be good for him.

The bell rings and I hold the phone with my shoulder and fold up my jacket, then drop it to the floor of the maintenance closet. I flip off the light. "I'll talk to you later. Nap time."

"Later," Holder says.

I end the call and set my alarm for fifty minutes later, then place my phone on the counter. I lower myself to the floor and lie down. I close my eyes and think about how much this year sucks. I hate that

Holder is going through what he's having to go through and there isn't a damn thing I can do about it. No one that close to me has ever died, much less someone as close as one of my sisters. A *twin* sister to be exact.

I don't even try to offer him advice, but I think he likes that. I think he needs me to just continue being myself, because God knows everyone else in this whole damn school has no clue how to act around him. If they weren't all such stupid assholes he'd probably still be here and school wouldn't suck half as bad as it does.

But it does suck. Everyone in this place sucks and I hate them all. I hate everybody but Holder and they're the reason he isn't here anymore.

I stretch my legs out in front of me and cross my ankles, then fold my arm over my eyes. At least I have fifth period.

Fifth period is nice.

• • •

My eyes flick open and I groan when something lands on me. I hear the sound of the door slam shut.

What the hell?

I place my hands on whatever just fell on me and begin to roll it off me when my hands graze a head full of soft hair.

It's a human?

A girl?

A chick just fell on me. In the maintenance closet. And she's crying.

"Who the hell are you?" I ask cautiously. Whoever she is, she tries to push off me but we both seem to be taking turns moving in the same direction. I lift up and try to roll her to my side but our heads crash together.

"Shit," she says.

I fall back onto my makeshift pillow and grab my forehead. "Sorry," I mumble.

Neither one of us moves this time. I can hear her sniffling, trying not to cry. I can't see two inches in front of me because the light is still out but I suddenly don't mind that she's still on top of me because she smells incredible.

"I think I'm lost," she says. "I thought I was walking into the bathroom."

I shake my head, even though I know she can't see it. "Not a bathroom," I say. "But why are you crying? Did you hurt yourself when you fell?"

I feel her whole body sigh on top of me. Even though I have no idea who she is or what she looks like, I can feel the sadness in her and it makes me a little sad in return. I'm not sure how it happens, but my arms go around her and her cheek falls against my chest. In the course of five seconds we go from extremely awkward to kind of comfortable, like we do this all the time.

It's weird and normal and hot and sad and strange and I don't really want to let go. It feels kind of euphoric, like we're in some sort of fairytale. Like she's Tinkerbell and I'm Peter Pan.

No, wait. I don't want to be Peter Pan.

Maybe she can be like Cinderella and I'll be her Prince Charming.

Yeah, I like that fantasy better. Cinderella's hot when she's all poor and sweaty and slaving over the stove. She also looks good in her ball gown. It also doesn't hurt that we're meeting in a broom closet. Very fitting.

I feel her pull a hand up to her face, more than likely wiping away a tear. "I hate them," she says softly.

"Who?"

"Everybody," she says. "I hate everybody."

I close my eyes and lift my hand, then run it down her hair, doing my best to comfort her. *Finally, someone who actually gets it.* I'm not sure why she hates everybody but I have a feeling she's got a pretty valid reason.

"I hate everybody too, Cinderella."

She laughs softly, probably confused as to why I just referred to her as Cinderella, but at least it's not more tears. Her laugh is intoxicating and I try to think of how I can get her to do it again. I'm trying to think of something funny to say when she lifts her face off my chest and I feel her scoot forward. Before I know it, I feel lips on mine and I'm not sure if I should shove her away or roll on top of her. I begin to lift my hands to her face, but she pulls back just as quick as she kissed me.

"Sorry," she says. "I should go." She places her palms beside me on the floor and starts to lift up, but I grab her face and pull her back down on top of me.

"No," I say. I bring her mouth back to mine and I kiss her. I keep our lips pressed firmly together as I lower her to my side. I pull her against me so that her head is resting on my jacket. Her breath tastes like Starburst and it makes me want to keep kissing her until I can identify every single flavor.

Her hand touches my arm and she gives it a tight squeeze just as my tongue slips inside her mouth. That would be strawberry on the tip of her tongue.

She keeps her hand on my arm, periodically moving it to the back of my head, then returning it to my arm. I keep my hand on her waist, never once moving it to touch any other part of her. The only thing we explore is each other's mouths. We kiss without making another sound. We kiss until the alarm sounds on my phone. Despite the noise, neither of us stops kissing. We don't even hesitate. We kiss for another solid minute until the bell rings in the hallway outside and suddenly lockers are slamming shut and people are talking and everything about our moment is stolen from us by all the inconvenient external factors of school.

I still my lips against hers, then slowly pull back.

"I have to get to class," she whispers.

I nod, even though she can't see me. "Me, too," I reply.

She begins to scoot out from beneath me. When I roll onto my back, I feel her move closer to me. Her mouth briefly meets mine one more time, then she pulls away and stands up. The second she opens the door, the light from the hallway pours in and I squeeze my eyes shut, throwing my arm over my face.

I hear the door shut behind her and by the time I adjust to the brightness, the light is gone again.

I sigh heavily. I also remain on the floor until my physical reaction to her subsides. I don't know who the hell she was or why the hell she ended up here, but I hope to God she comes back. I need a whole hell of a lot more of that.

. . .

She didn't come back the next day. Or the day after that. In fact, today marks exactly a week since she literally fell into my arms, and I've convinced myself that maybe that whole day was a dream. I did stay up most of the night before watching zombie movies with Chunk, but even though I was going on two hours of sleep, I don't know that I would have been able to imagine that. My fantasies aren't that fun.

Whether she comes back or not, I still don't have a fifth period and until someone calls me out on it, I'll keep hiding out in here. I actually slept way too much last night, so I'm not tired. I pull my phone out to text Holder when the door to the closet begins to open.

"Are you in here, kid?" I hear her whisper.

My heart immediately picks up pace and I can't tell if it's that she came back or if it's because the light is on and I'm not really sure I want to see what she looks like when she opens this door.

"I'm here," I say.

The door is still barely cracked. She slips a hand inside and slides it around the wall until she finds the light, then she flicks it off. The door opens and she slips into the room, then quickly shuts it behind her.

"Can I hide with you?" she asks. Her voice sounds a little different than last time. It sounds happier.

"You're not crying today," I say.

I feel her make her way over to me. She grazes my leg and can feel that I'm seated on a countertop, so she feels around me until she finds a clear spot. She pushes herself up beside me and takes a seat next to me.

"I'm not sad today," she says, her voice much closer this time.

"Good." It's quiet for several seconds, but it's nice. I'm not sure why she came back or why it took her a week, but I'm glad she's here.

"Why were you in here last week?" she asks. "And why are you in here now?"

"Schedule mishap. I was never assigned a fifth period, so I hide out and hope administration doesn't notice."

She laughs. "Smart."

"Yep."

It's quiet again for a minute or so. Our hands are gripping the edge of the counter and every time she swings her legs, her fingers barely touch mine. I eventually just move my hand on top of hers and pull it onto my lap. It seems odd to just grab her hand like this, but we pretty much made out for fifteen minutes straight last week so holding hands is actually reversing a base.

She slides her fingers between mine and our palms meet, then

I fold my fingers over hers. "This is nice," she says. "I've never held anyone's hand before."

I freeze.

How the hell old is she?

"You're not in junior high, are you?"

"*God* no. I've just never held anyone's hand before. The guys I've been with seem to forget this part. But it's nice. I like it."

"Yeah," I agree. "It is nice."

"Wait," she says. "*You* aren't in junior high, are you?"

"No. Not yet," I say.

She swings her leg out to the side and kicks me, then we both laugh.

"This is kind of weird, isn't it?" she asks.

"Elaborate. Lots of things could be considered weird, so I'm not sure what you're referring to."

I feel her shoulders shrug. "I don't know. This. Us. Kissing and talking and holding hands and we don't even know what the other looks like."

"I'm really good looking," I say.

She laughs.

"I'm serious. If you could see me right now, you'd be on your knees begging me to be your boyfriend so you could flaunt me around the school."

"Highly unlikely," she says. "I don't do boyfriends. Overrated."

"If you don't hold hands and you don't do boyfriends, then what *do* you do?"

She sighs. "Pretty much everything else. I've got quite a reputation, you know. In fact, it's possible the two of us may have had sex before and we don't even realize it."

"Not possible. You'd remember me."

She laughs again and as much as I'm having fun talking to her, that laugh makes me want to drag her to the floor with me and do nothing but kiss her again.

"Are you actually good looking?" she asks skeptically.

"Terribly good looking," I reply.

"Let me guess. Dark hair, brown eyes, great abs, white teeth, Abercrombie & Fitch."

"Close," I say. "*Light* brown hair, correct on the eyes, abs, and teeth, but American Eagle Outfitters all the way."

"Impressive," she says.

"My turn," I say. "Thick blonde hair, big blue eyes, an adorable little white dress with a matching hat, royal blue skin, and you're about two feet tall."

She laughs loudly. "You have a thing for Smurfette?"

"A guy can dream."

The sound of her laughter actually makes my heart hurt. It hurts because I really want to know who this chick is but I know once I find out, I more than likely won't want her like I want her right now.

She inhales a breath and then the room becomes quiet. So quiet, it's almost uncomfortable.

"I'm not coming back in here after today," she says softly.

I squeeze her hand, surprised by the sadness I feel at that confession.

"I'm moving. Not right away, but soon. This summer. I just think it'd be silly if I came back here, because eventually we'll have to turn on the light or we'll slip up and say our names and I just don't think I want to know who you are."

I graze my thumb over her hand. "Why'd you come back today, then?"

She exhales a delicate breath. "I wanted to thank you."

"For what? Kissing you? That's all I did."

"Yeah," she says, matter-of-fact. "Exactly. For kissing me. For *just* kissing me. Do you know how long it's been since a guy has actually *just* kissed me? After I left last week I tried to remember, but I couldn't. Every time a guy has ever kissed me, he's always been in such a hurry to move on to what comes after the kisses that I don't think anyone has ever taken the time to give me an honest to God, genuine kiss before."

I shake my head. "That's really depressing," I say. "But don't give me too much credit. I've been known to want to rush past that part in the past. I just didn't really care to rush past it last week because you're a pretty phenomenal kisser."

"Yeah," she says confidently. "I know. Imagine what making love to me could feel like."

I swallow the sudden lump in my throat. "Believe me, I have. For about seven days straight now."

Her legs stop swinging next to me. I don't know if I just made her uncomfortable with that comment.

"You know what else is sad?" she asks. "No one's ever made love to me before."

This conversation is headed in a weird direction. I can already tell.

"You're young. Plenty of time for that. Virginity is actually a turn-on, so you have nothing to worry about."

She laughs, but it's a sad laugh this time.

Weird how I can already differentiate her laughs.

"I am *so* not a virgin," she says. "That's why it's sad. I'm pretty skilled in the sex department, but looking back . . . I've never loved any of them. None of them have ever loved me, either. Sometimes I wonder if sex with someone who actually loves you is different. Better."

I think about her question and realize that I don't have an answer. I've never loved anyone, either. "Good question," I say. "It's kind of sad that we've both had sex, multiple times it sounds like, but neither of us has ever loved anyone we've done it with. Says a lot about our characters, don't you think?"

"Yeah," she says quietly. "Sure does. A lot of sad truth."

It's quiet for a while and I still have hold of her hand. I can't stop thinking about the fact that no one's ever held her hand before. It makes me wonder if I've ever held the hands of any of the girls I've had sex with. Not that there have been a ton, but enough that I should be able to recall holding one of their hands.

"I might be one of those guys," I ashamedly admit. "I don't know if I've ever held a girl's hand before."

"You're holding mine," she says.

I nod slowly. "So I am."

A few more beats of silence pass before she speaks again.

"What if I leave here in forty-five minutes and never hold another guy's hand again? What if I go through life like I am right now? What if guys continue to take me for granted and I do nothing to change it and I'll have lots of sex, but never know what it's like to make love?"

"So don't do that. Find you a good guy and tie him down and make love to him every night."

She groans. "That terrifies me. As curious as I am about the difference between making love and having sex, my stance on relationships makes it impossible to find out."

I think about her comment for a while. It's weird, because she sounds a little like the female version of me. I'm not sure I'm as opposed to relationships as she is, but I've definitely never told a girl I loved her and I really hope that doesn't happen for a hell of a long time.

"You're really never coming back?" I ask.

"I'm really not coming back," she says.

I let go of her hand and press my palms onto the cabinet, then jump down. I move and stand in front of her, then place my hands on either side of her. "Let's solve our dilemma right now."

She leans back. "Which dilemma?"

I move my hands and place them on her hips, then pull her to me. "We have a good forty-five minutes to work with. I'm pretty sure I could make love to you in forty-five minutes. We can see what it's like and if it's even worth going through relationships in the future. That way when you leave here, you won't worry about never knowing what it's like."

She laughs nervously, then leans toward me again. "How do you make love to someone you aren't in love with?"

I lean forward until my mouth is next to her ear. "We pretend."

I can hear the breath catch in her lungs. She turns her face slightly toward mine and I feel her lips graze my cheek. "What if we're bad actors?" she whispers.

I close my eyes, because the possibility that I might actually be making love to this chick in a matter of minutes is almost too much to take in.

"You should audition for me," she says. "If you're convincing then I just might agree to this absurd idea of yours."

"Deal," I say.

I take a step back and remove my shirt, then lay it on the floor. I grab my jacket off the counter and unfold it, then lay it on the floor as well. I turn back to the counter, then scoop her up. She locks herself around me, burying her head in my neck.

"Where's your shirt?" she asks, running her hands across my shoulder. I lower her to the floor, onto her back. I ease myself to her side and pull her against me.

"You're lying on it," I respond.

"Oh," she says. "That was considerate of you."

I bring my hand up to her cheek. "That's what people do when they're this in love."

I feel her smile. "How in love are we?"

"All the way," I say.

"Why? What is it about me you love so much?"

"Your laugh," I say immediately, not sure how much of that is actually made up. "I love your humor. I also love the way you tuck your hair behind your ears when you're reading. And I love how you hate to talk on the phone almost as much as I do. I really love that you leave me those little notes all the time in your adorable handwriting. And I love that you love my dog so much, because he really likes you. I also love taking showers with you. Those are always fun."

I slide my hand from her cheek to the nape of her neck. I ease my mouth forward and rest my lips against hers.

"Wow," she says against my mouth. "You're really convincing."

I smile and pull away. "Stop breaking character," I tease. "Now it's your turn. What do you love about me?"

"I do love your dog," she says. "He's a great dog. I also love how you open doors for me even though I'm supposed to want to open doors for myself. I love that you don't try to pretend you like old black and white movies like everyone else does, because they bore the hell out of me. I also love it when I'm at your house and every time your parents turn the other way, you steal little kisses from me. My favorite part about you though is when I catch you staring at me. I love that you don't look away and you stare unapologetically, like you aren't ashamed that you can't stop watching me. It's all you want to do because you think I'm the most amazing thing you've ever laid eyes on. I love how much you love me."

"You're absolutely right," I whisper. "I love staring at you."

I kiss her mouth, then trail kisses across her cheek and up her jawline. I press my lips against her ear and even though I know we're pretending, my mouth runs dry at the thought of the words about to pass my lips. I hesitate, almost deciding against it. But an even bigger part of me wants to say it. A huge part of me wishes I could mean it and a small part of me thinks I probably could.

I run my hands up and through her hair. "I love you," I whisper.

The next breath she draws in is a deep one. My heart is hammering against my chest and I'm quiet, waiting on her next move. I have no idea what comes next. Then again, neither does she.

Her hands move from my shoulders and slowly make their way up to my neck. She tilts her head until her mouth is flush against my ear. "I love you more," she whispers. I can feel the smile on her lips and I wonder if it matches the smile on my face. I don't know why I'm suddenly enjoying this so much, but I am.

"You're so beautiful," I whisper, moving my lips closer to her mouth. "So damn beautiful. And every single one of those guys who somehow passed this up is a complete fool."

She closes the gap between our lips and I kiss her, but this time the kiss seems so much more intimate. For a brief moment, I actually feel like I really do love all those things about her and she really does love all those things about me. We're kissing and touching and pulling the rest of our clothes off in such a hurry, it feels as if we're on a timer.

I guess we technically are.

I pull my wallet out of the pocket of my jeans and grab a condom, then ease myself back against her.

"You can change your mind," I whisper, hoping to hell she doesn't.

"So can you," she says.

I laugh.

She laughs.

Then we both shut the hell up and spend the rest of the hour proving exactly how much we love each other.

•   •   •

I'm on my knees now, quietly gathering our clothes. After I slip my shirt over my head, I pull her up and help her with her own shirt. I stand up and pull on my jeans, then help her to her feet. I rest my chin on top of her head and pull her against me, recognizing the perfect fit.

"I could turn on the light before you leave," I say. "Aren't you a little curious to see the face of the guy you're madly in love with?"

She shakes her head against my chest with her laugh. "It'll ruin everything," she says. Her words are muffled by my shirt, so she lifts her head away from my chest and tilts her face up to mine. "Let's not ruin it. Once we find out who the other is, we'll find something we don't like. Maybe *lots* of things we don't like. Right now it's perfect. We can always have this perfect memory of that one time we loved somebody."

I kiss her again, but it doesn't last long because the bell rings. She doesn't release her hold from around my waist. She just presses her head against my chest again and squeezes me tighter. "I need to go," she says.

I close my eyes and nod. "I know."

I'm surprised by just how much I don't want her to go, knowing I'll never see her again. I almost beg her to stay, but I also know she's right. It only feels perfect because we're *pretending* it's perfect.

She begins to pull away from me, so I lift my hands to her cheeks one last time. "I love you, babe. Wait for me after school, okay? In our usual spot."

"You know I'll be there," she says. "And I love you, too." She stands on her tiptoes and presses her lips to mine—hard and desperate and sad. She pulls away and makes her way to the door. As soon as she begins to open it, I walk swiftly to her and push the door shut with my hand. I press my chest against her back and I lower my mouth to her ear.

"I wish it could be real," I whisper. I put my hand on the doorknob and open it, then turn my head when she slips out the door.

I sigh and run my hands through my hair. I think I need a few minutes before I can leave this room. I'm not sure I want to forget the way she smells just yet. In fact, I stand here in the dark and try my hardest to commit every single thing about her to my memory, since that's the only place I'll ever see her again.

Chapter One

"Oh, my *God*!" I say, frustrated. "Lighten up." I crank the car just as Val climbs inside and slams her door in a huff, then pushes herself back against the seat.

As soon as she's inside the car, the overwhelming amount of perfume she has on begins to suffocate me. I crack the window, but just enough so that she won't think I'm insulting her. She knows how much perfume bothers me, especially when chicks smell like they bathe in it, but she never seems to care what I think, because she continues to douse it on by the gallon.

"You're so immature, Daniel," she mutters. She flips the visor down and pulls her lipstick from her purse, then begins to reapply it. "I'm beginning to wonder if you'll *ever* change."

Change?

What the hell is *that* supposed to mean?

"Why would I change?" I ask, cocking my head out of curiosity.

She sighs and drops her lipstick back into her purse, smacks her lips together, then turns toward me. "So you're telling me you're happy with the way you act?"

What?

With the way *I* act? Is she really commenting on the way *I* act? The same girl I've seen curse at waitresses for something as simple as too much ice in her glass is seriously commenting on the way *I* act?

I've been seeing her off and on for months now and I haven't had a single clue that she was hoping I would eventually change. Hoping I'd become someone I'm not.

Come to think of it, I keep getting back together with her, thinking *she'll* be the one to change. To be *nice* for once. In reality, people are who they are and they'll never really change. So why the hell are Val and I even wasting our time on this exhausting relationship if we don't even really like who the other is?

"I didn't think so," she says smugly, incorrectly assuming my silence was admission that I'm not happy with how I act. In actuality, my silence was the moment of clarity I've needed since the day I met her.

I remain silent until we pull into her driveway. I leave the car running, indicating that I have no plans on going inside with her tonight.

"You're leaving?" she asks.

I nod and stare out the driver's side window. I don't want to look at her, because I'm a guy and she's hot and I know if I look at her, then my moment of clarity regarding our relationship will become foggy and I'll end up inside her house, making up with her on her bed like I always do.

"You aren't the one who gets to be mad, Daniel. You acted ridiculous tonight. And in front of my parents, no less! How do you expect them to ever approve of you if you act the way you do?"

I have to exhale a slow, calming breath so that I don't raise my voice like she's doing right now. "How do I act, Val? Because I was myself at dinner tonight, just like I'm myself every other minute of the day."

"Exactly!" she says. "There's a time and a place for your stupid nicknames and immature antics and dinner with my parents isn't the time *or* the place!"

I rub my hands over my face out of frustration, then I turn and look at her. "This is me," I say, gesturing toward myself. "If you don't like all of me, then we've got serious issues, Val. I'm not changing and honestly, it wouldn't be fair of me to ask you to change, either. I would never ask you to pretend to be something you're not, which is exactly what you're asking of me right now. I'm *not* changing, I'll *never* change and I would really like it if you would get the hell out of my car right now because your perfume is making me fucking nauseous."

Her eyes narrow and she grabs her purse off the console and pulls it toward her. "Oh, that's nice, Daniel. Insult my perfume to get back at me. See what I mean? You're the epitome of immature." She opens the car door and unbuckles her seatbelt.

"Well at least I'm not asking you to *change* your perfume," I say mockingly.

She shakes her head. "I can't do this anymore," she says, getting out of the car. "We're done, Daniel. For good this time."

"Thank *God*," I say loud enough for her to hear me. She slams her door and marches toward her house. I roll down her window to air out the perfume and I back out of the driveway.

Where the hell is Holder? If I don't get to complain to someone about her, I'll fucking scream.

•　　•　　•

I climb into Sky's window and she's sitting on the floor, rummaging through pictures. She looks up and smiles as I make my way into her room. "Hey, Daniel," she says.

"Hey, Cheese Tits," I say as I drop down onto her bed. "Where's your hopeless boyfriend?"

She nudges her head toward her bedroom door. "They're in the kitchen making ice cream. You want some?"

"Nah," I say. "I'm too heartbroken to eat anything right now."

"Val having a bad day?"

"Val's having a bad *life*," I say. "And after tonight I've finally realized I don't want to be a part of it."

She raises her eyebrows. "Oh, yeah? Sounds serious this time."

I shrug. "We broke up an hour ago. And who's *they*?"

She shoots me a confused look, so I clarify my question. "You said *they* were in the kitchen making ice cream. Who's *they*?"

Sky opens her mouth to answer me when her bedroom door swings open and Holder walks in with two bowls of ice cream in his hands. A girl is following behind him with her own bowl of ice cream and a spoon hanging out of her mouth. She pulls the spoon from her lips and kicks the bedroom door shut with her foot, then turns toward the bed and stops when she sees me.

She looks vaguely familiar, but I can't place her. Which is odd because she's cute as hell and I feel like I should probably know her name or remember where I've seen her, but I don't.

She walks to the bed and sits down on the opposite end of it, eyeing me the whole time. She dips her spoon into her ice cream, then puts the spoon back in her mouth.

I can't stop staring at that spoon. I think I love that spoon.

"What are you doing here?" Holder asks. I regretfully take my eyes off the Ice Cream Girl and watch as he takes a seat on the floor next to Sky and picks up a few of the pictures.

"I'm done with her, Holder," I say, stretching my legs out in front of me on the bed. "For good. She's fucking crazy."

"But I thought that's why you loved her," he says mockingly.

I roll my eyes. "Thanks for the insight, Dr. Shitmitten."

Sky takes one of the pictures out of Holder's hands. "I think he's actually serious this time," she says to him. "No more Val." Sky tries to look sad for my sake, but I know she's relieved. Val never really fit in with the two of them. Now that I think about it, she never really fit in with me, either.

Holder looks up at me curiously. "Done for good? Really?" He sounds oddly impressed.

"Yeah, *really*, really."

"Who's Val?" Ice Cream Girl asks. "Or better yet, who are *you*?"

"Oh, my bad," Sky interrupts. She points back and forth between Ice Cream Girl and me. "Six, this is Dean's best friend, Daniel. Daniel, this is my best friend, Six."

I'll never get used to hearing Sky call him Dean, but her introduction gives me an excuse to look over at that spoon again. Six pulls it out of her mouth and points it at me. "Nice to meet you, Daniel," she says.

How in the hell can I steal that spoon before she leaves?

"Why does your name sound familiar?" I ask her.

She shrugs. "I dunno. Maybe because six is a fairly common number? Either that or you've heard of what a raging whore I am."

I laugh. I don't know why, though, because her comment really wasn't funny. It was actually a little disturbing. "No, that's not it," I say, still confused as to why her name sounds so familiar. I don't think Sky has ever mentioned her in front of me before.

"The party last year," Holder says, forcing me to look at him again. I'm pretty sure I roll my eyes when I have to look away from her, but I don't mean to. I'd just much rather stare at her than at Holder. "Remember?" he says. "It was the week I got back from Austin and a few days before I met Sky. The night Grayson pummeled you on the floor for saying you took Sky's virginity?"

"Oh, you mean the night you pulled me off of him before I even got the chance to kick his ass?" It still irritates me just thinking about it. I could have had him if Holder hadn't stepped in.

"Yeah," Holder confirms. "Jaxon mentioned something that night about Sky and Six, but I didn't know who they were at the time. I think that's where you heard her name."

"Wait, wait, wait," Sky says, waving her hands in the air and looking at me like I'm crazy. "What do you mean Grayson pummeled you because you said you took my *virginity*? What the *hell*, Daniel?"

Holder puts a reassuring hand on Sky's lower back. "It's cool, babe. He just said it to piss Grayson off because I was about to kick the idiot's ass for the way he was talking about you."

Sky is shaking her head, still confused. "But you didn't even know me. You just said it was a few days before you met me, so why would you be pissed that Grayson was talking shit about me?"

I stare at Holder, too, waiting for his answer. I never thought about it then, but that is odd that he was pissed over Grayson's comments when he didn't even know Sky at the time.

"I didn't like how he was talking about you," he says, leaning in to kiss Sky on the side of the head. "It made me think he probably talked about Les the same way and it pissed me off."

Shit. Of course he would think that. Now I *really* wish he had let me kick Grayson's ass that night.

"That's sweet, Holder," Six says. "You were protecting her before you even knew her."

Holder laughs. "Oh, you don't know the half of it, Six."

Sky looks up at him and they smile at each other, almost like they have some sort of secret, then they both turn their attention back to the pictures on the floor in front of them.

"What are those?" I ask, inquiring about the pictures they're looking through.

"For the yearbook," Six says, answering me. She sets the bowl of ice cream on the bed beside her, then pulls her feet up and sits cross-legged. "Apparently we're supposed to submit pictures of ourselves as kids for the senior page, so Sky is going through the pics Karen gave her."

"You go to the same school as us?" I ask, referring to the fact that she included herself in the explanation of the assignment. I know we go to a huge school, but I have a feeling I would remember her, especially if she's Sky's best friend.

"I haven't been to that school since junior year," she says. "But I'll be there once Monday rolls around." She says it like she's not at all looking forward to it.

I can't help but smile at her reply, though. I wouldn't mind having to see this girl on a recurring basis. "So does that mean you'll be joining our lunchroom alliance?" I lean forward and grab the bowl of ice cream she didn't finish. I pull it to me and take a bite.

She watches me as I close my lips around the spoon and pull it out of my mouth. She scrunches up her nose, staring at the spoon. "I could have herpes, you know," she says.

I grin at her and wink. "You somehow just made herpes sound appealing."

She laughs, but her bowl is suddenly ripped from my hands by Holder and he's pulling me off the bed. My feet hit the floor and he shoves me toward the window. "Go home, Daniel," he says, releasing his grip on my shirt as he lowers himself back to the floor next to Sky.

"What the *hell*, man?" I yell.

Seriously, though. *What the hell?*

"She's Sky's best friend," he says, waving a hand in Six's direction. "You're not allowed to flirt with her. If the two of you mess around it'll just cause tension and make things weird and I don't want that. Now leave and don't come back until you can be around her without having the perverted thoughts I know are going through your head right now."

For the first time in my life, I think I'm actually speechless. Perhaps I should nod and agree with him, but the idiot just made the biggest mistake he could possibly make.

"Shit, Holder," I groan, running my palms down my face. "Why the hell did you have to go and *do* that? You just made her off-limits, man." I begin to make my way back out the window. Once I'm outside, I stick my head back through and look at him. "You should have told me I should date her, then I more than likely wouldn't have been interested. But you had to go and make her forbidden, didn't you?"

"Gee, Daniel," Six says, unenthusiastically. "Glad to know you think of me as a human being and not a challenge." She looks at Holder as she stands up from the bed. "And I didn't realize I had a fifth overprotective brother," she says, making her way toward the window. "I'll see you guys later. I probably need to go rummage through my own pictures before Monday, anyway."

Holder glances back at me as I step aside and allow Six to climb out the window. He doesn't say anything, but the look he gives me is a silent warning that Six is completely off-limits to me. I raise my hands in defense, then pull the window shut after Six is outside. She walks a few feet to the house next door and begins to climb through that window.

"Do you take shortcuts through windows all the time, or do you happen to live in that house?" I ask, walking toward her. Once she's inside, she spins around and leans her head out. "This would be *my* window," she says. "And don't even think about following me inside. This window has been out of commission for almost a year and I have no plans to reopen for business."

She tucks her shoulder-length blonde hair behind her ears and I take a step back, hoping a little distance will allow my heart to stop attacking the walls of my chest. But now all I want to do is figure out a way to recommission her window.

"You really have four older brothers?"

She nods. I hate the fact that she has four older brothers, but only because it presents four more reasons why I shouldn't date her. Add that to Holder making her off-limits and I know she's the only thing I'll be able to think about now.

Thanks, Holder. Thanks a lot.

She rests her chin in her hands and stares at me. It's dark outside, but the moon overhead is casting a light right on her face and she looks like a fucking angel. I don't even know if people should use the words *fucking* and *angel* in the same thought structure, but *shit*. She really looks like a fucking angel with her blonde hair and big eyes. I'm not even sure what color her eyes are because it's dark and I didn't really pay attention when we were in Sky's bedroom, but whatever color they are, it's my new favorite color.

"You're very charismatic," she says.

Jesus. Her voice completely slays me. "Thanks. You're pretty cute yourself."

"I didn't say you were cute, Daniel. I said you were charismatic. There's a difference."

"Not much of one," I say. "You like Italian?"

She frowns and pulls back a few inches like I just insulted her. "Why would you ask me that?"

Her reaction confuses me. I have no idea how that comment could have offended her. "Uh, have you never been asked out on a date before?"

The scowl disappears from her face and she leans forward again. "Oh. You mean food. I'm sort of tired of Italian food, actually. Just got back from a seven-month exchange there. If you're asking me out on a date, I'd rather have sushi."

"I've never had sushi," I admit, trying to process the fact that I'm pretty sure she just agreed to go out on a date with me.

"When?"

This was way too easy. I figured she'd put up a fight and make me beg a little like Val always does. I love that she isn't playing games. She's straightforward and I like that about her already.

"I can't take you tonight," I say. "I had my heart completely broken about an hour ago by a psychotic bitch and I need a little more time to recover from that relationship. How about tomorrow night?"

"Tomorrow is Sunday," she says.

"Do you have an issue with Sundays?"

"Not really, I guess. It just seems odd to go on a first date on a Sunday night. Meet me here at seven o'clock, then."

"I'll meet you at your front door," I say. "And you might not want to tell Sky where you're going unless you want to see me get my ass kicked."

"What's to tell?" she says sarcastically. "It's not like we're going on a random Sunday night date or anything."

I smile and back away, slowly heading backward to my car. "It was nice to meet you, Six."

She places her hand on her window to pull it down. "Likewise. I think."

I laugh, then turn to head toward my car. I'm almost to the door when she calls my name. I spin back around and she's leaning out her window.

"I'm sorry about your broken heart," she whispers loudly. She ducks back into her bedroom and the window closes.

What broken heart? I'm pretty sure this is the first time my heart has actually felt any form of relief since the moment I started dating Val.

Chapter Two

"Does this look okay?" I ask Chunk when I make it into the kitchen. She turns and looks me up and down, then shrugs.

"I guess. Where ya going?"

I step in front of one of the mirrors lining the hallway and check my hair again. "A date."

She groans, then turns back around to the table in front of her. "You've never cared before what you look like. You better not be proposing to her. I'll divorce this family before I allow you to make her my sister."

My mother walks past me and pats me on the shoulder. "You look great, honey. I wouldn't wear those shoes, though."

I look down at my shoes. "Why? What's wrong with my shoes?"

She opens a cabinet, takes out a pan, then turns to face me. Her eyes fall to my shoes again. "They're too bright." She turns and walks to the stove. "Shoes should never be neon."

"They're yellow. Not neon."

"*Neon* yellow," Chunk says.

"Not saying I think they're ugly," my mother says. "I just know Val, and Val is more than likely going to hate your shoes."

I walk to the kitchen counter and grab my keys, then put my cell phone in my pocket. "I don't give a shit what Val thinks."

My mother turns and looks at me curiously. "Well you're asking your thirteen-year-old sister if you look good enough for your date, so I think you kind of *do* care what Val thinks."

"I'm not going out with Val. I broke up with Val. I have a new date tonight."

Chunk's arms go up in the air and she looks up to the ceiling. "Thank the *Lord*!" she proclaims loudly.

My mother laughs and nods. "Yes. Thank the Lord," she says, relieved. She turns back toward the stove and I can't stop looking back and forth between the both of them.

"What? Neither of you like Val?" I know Val is a bitch, but my family seemed to like her. Especially my mom. I honestly thought she'd be upset we broke up.

"I hate Val," Chunk says.

"God, me, too," my mother groans.

"Me three," my father says, walking past me.

None of them are looking at me, but they're all responding like this has been a previously discussed topic.

"You mean all of you hated Val?"

My father turns to face me. "Your mother and I are masters at reverse psychology, Danny-boy. Don't act so surprised."

Chunk raises her hand in the air toward my father. "Me, too, Dad. I reverse psychologized him, too."

My dad reaches over and high-fives Chunk's hand. "Well played, Chunk."

I lean against the frame of the door and stare at them. "You guys were just pretending to like Val? What the hell for?"

My dad sits at the table and picks up a newspaper. "Children are naturally inclined to make choices that will displease their parents. If we had told you how we really felt about Val, you probably would have ended up marrying her just to spite us. Which is why we pretended to love her."

Assholes. All three of them. "You're never meeting another one of my girlfriends again."

My father chuckles, but doesn't seem at all disappointed.

"Who is she?" Chunk asks. "The girl you're actually making an effort for."

"None of your damn business," I reply. "Now that I know how this family works, I'm never bringing her around any of you."

I turn to head out the door and my mother calls after me. "Well if it helps, we already love her, Daniel! She's a sweetheart!"

"And beautiful," my dad says. "She's a keeper!"

I shake my head. "Y'all suck."

•   •   •

"You're late," Six says when she appears at her front door. She walks out of her house with her back to me, inserting her key in the lock.

"You don't want me to meet your parents?" I ask, wondering why she's locking her door this early in the evening. She turns around and faces me.

"They're old. They ate dinner like ten hours ago and went to bed at seven."

Blue. Her eyes are blue.

Holy shit, she's cute. Her hair is lighter than I thought it was last night in Sky's room. Her skin is flawless. It's like she's the same girl from last night, only now she's in HD. And I was right. She really does look like a fucking angel.

She steps out of the way and I shut the screen door, still unable to take my eyes off her. "I actually got here early," I say, finally replying to her first comment. "Holder was dropping Sky off at her house and I swear it took them half an hour to say their good-byes. I had to wait until the coast was clear."

She slides her house key into her back pocket and nods. "Ready?"

I eye her up and down. "Did you forget your purse?"

She shakes her head. "Nope. I hate purses." She pats her back pocket. "All I need is my house key. I didn't bother bringing money since this date was your idea. You're paying, right?"

Whoa.

Back up.

Let's assess the last thirty seconds, shall we?

She hates purses. That means she didn't bring makeup. Which means she won't constantly be reapplying that shit like Val does. It also means she's not hiding a gallon of perfume anywhere on her person. And it also means she had no plans at all to offer to pay for her half of dinner, which seems a little old-fashioned, but for some reason I like it.

"I love that you don't carry a purse," I say.

"I love that you don't carry one, either," she says with a laugh.

"I do. It's in my car," I say, nudging my head toward my car.

She laughs again and begins walking toward the porch steps. I do the same until I see Sky standing just inside her room with her window wide open. I immediately grab Six by her shoulders and pull her until both of our backs are flat against the front door. "You can see Sky's window from the front yard. She'll see us."

Six glances up at me. "You're really taking this *off-limits* order seriously," she says in a hushed voice.

"I *have* to," I whisper. "Holder doesn't kid around when he forbids me to date people."

She arches a curious eyebrow. "Does Holder usually dictate who you can and can't date?"

"No. You're actually the first."

"Then how do you know he'll actually get mad over it?"

I shrug. "I don't, really. But the thought of hiding it from him just seems sort of fun. Is it not a little bit exciting for you, hiding this date from Sky?"

"Yeah," she says with a shrug. "I guess it is."

Our backs are still pressed against the door and for some reason, we're still whispering. It's not like Sky could hear us from here, but again, the whispering makes it more fun. And I really like the sound of Six's voice when she whispers.

"How do you propose we get out of this situation, Six?"

"Well," she says, pondering my question for a moment. "Normally when I'm attempting a risky, clandestine, secret date and I need to escape my house undetected, I ask myself, 'What would MacGyver do?'"

Oh, my god, this chick just mentioned MacGyver?

Hell.

Yes.

I break my eyes away from hers long enough to hide the fact that I think I just fell for her and also to assess our escape route. I glance at the swing on the porch, then look back at Six when I'm sure the cheesy grin is gone from my face.

"I think MacGyver would take your porch swing and build an invisible force field out of grass and matches. Then he would attach a jet engine to it and fly it out of here undetected. Unfortunately I'm all out of matches."

"Hmmm," she says, squinting her eyes like she's coming up with some brilliant plan. "That's an unfortunate inconvenience." She glances toward my car parked in her driveway, then back up to me. "We could just crawl to your car so she doesn't see us."

And a brilliant plan it would be if it didn't involve a girl getting dirty. I've learned in my six months of on-again off-again with Val that girls like to stay clean.

"You'll get dirt on your hands," I warn her. "I don't think you can walk into a fancy sushi restaurant with dirty hands and jeans."

She looks down at her jeans, then back up to me. "I know this great Bar-B-Q restaurant we could go to, instead. The floor is covered in discarded peanut shells. One time I saw this really fat guy eating at a booth and he wasn't even wearing a shirt."

I smile at the same time I fall a little harder for her. "Sounds perfect."

We both drop to our hands and knees and crawl our way off her porch. She's giggling, and the sound of it makes me laugh. "Shh," I whisper when we reach the bottom of the steps. We crawl across the yard in a hurry, both of us glancing toward Sky's house every few feet. Once we reach the car, I reach up to my door handle. "Crawl through the driver's side," I say to her. "She'll be less likely to see you."

I open the door for her and she crawls into the front seat. Once she's inside the car, I climb in after her and slide into my seat. We're both crouched down, which is pointless if you think about it. If Sky were to look out her bedroom window, she'd see my car parked in Six's driveway. It wouldn't matter if she saw our heads or not.

Six wipes the dirt from her hands onto the legs of her jeans and it completely turns me on. She turns her head to face me and I'm still staring at the dirt smeared across the thighs of her jeans. I somehow tear my gaze away and look her in the eyes.

"You'll have to disguise your car next time you come over," she says. "This is way too risky."

I like her comment a little too much.

"Confident there'll be a next time already?" I ask, smirking at her. "The date just started."

"Good point," she says with a shrug. "I might hate you by the end of the date."

"Or I might hate *you*," I say.

"Impossible." She props her foot up on the dash. "I'm unhateable."

"Unhateable isn't even a real word."

She peers over her shoulder into the backseat, then faces forward again with a scowl. "Why does it smell like you had a harem of whores in here?" She pulls her shirt up over her nose to cover up the smell.

"Does it still smell like perfume?" I don't even smell it anymore. It's probably seeped into my pores and I'm now immune to it.

She nods. "It's awful," she says, her voice muffled by her shirt. "Roll down a window." She makes a fake spitting sound like she's trying to get the taste of it out of her mouth and it makes me laugh.

I crank the car, then put it in reverse and begin to back out.

"The wind will mess up your hair if I roll down the windows. You didn't bring a purse, which means you didn't bring a brush, which means you won't be able to fix your hair when we get to the restaurant."

She reaches to her door and presses the button to roll down her window. "I'm already dirty and I'd rather have messy hair than smell like a harem," she says. She rolls the window down completely, then motions for me to roll mine down as well, so I do.

I put the car in drive and press on the gas. The car immediately fills with wind and fresh air and her hair begins flying around in all directions, but she just relaxes into the seat.

"Much better," she says, grinning at me. She closes her eyes while inhaling a deep breath of the fresh air.

I try to pay attention to the road, but she makes it pretty damn hard.

• • •

"What are your brothers' names?" I ask her. "Are they numbers, too?"

"Zachary, Michael, Aaron, and Evan. I'm ten years younger than the youngest."

"Were you an accident?"

She nods. "The best kind. My mother was forty-two when she had me, but they were excited when I came out a girl."

"I'm glad you came out a girl."

She laughs. "Me, too."

"Why'd they name you Six if you were actually the fifth child?"

"Six isn't my name," she says. "Full name is Seven Marie Jacobs, but I got mad at them for moving me to Texas when I was fourteen so I started calling myself Six to piss them off. They didn't really care, but I was stubborn and refused to give up. Now everyone calls me Six but them."

I love that she gave herself a nickname. My kind of girl.

"Question still applies," I say. "Why did they name you *Seven* if you were actually the fifth child?"

"No reason, really. My dad just liked the number."

I nod, then take a bite of food, eyeing her carefully. I'm waiting for that moment. The one that always comes with girls, where the pedestal you place them on in the beginning gets kicked out from under them. It's usually the moment they start talking about ex-boyfriends or mention how many kids they want or they do something really annoying, like apply lipstick in the middle of dinner.

I've been waiting patiently for Six's flaws to stand out, but so far I can't find any. Granted, we've only interacted with each other for a collective three or four hours now, so hers may just be buried deeper than other people's.

"So you're a middle child?" she asks. "Do you suffer from middle-child syndrome?"

I shake my head. "Probably about as much as you suffer from fifth-child syndrome. Besides, Hannah is four years older than me and Chunk is five years younger, so we have a nice spread."

She chokes on her drink with her laugh. "Chunk? You call your little sister Chunk?"

"We all call her Chunk. She was a fat baby."

"You have nicknames for everyone," she says. "You call Sky

Cheese Tits. You call Holder *Hopeless*. What do you call me when I'm not around?"

"If I give people nicknames, I do it to their faces," I point out. "And I haven't figured yours out yet." I lean back in my seat and wonder myself why I haven't given her one yet. The nicknames I give people are usually pretty instant.

"Is it a bad thing you haven't nicknamed me yet?"

I shrug. "Not really. I'm just still trying to figure you out is all. You're kind of contradictory."

She arches an eyebrow. "I'm contradictory? In what ways?"

"All of them. You're cute as hell, but you don't give a shit what you look like. You look sweet, but I have a feeling you're just the right mix of good and evil. You seem really easygoing, like you aren't the type to play games with guys, but you're kind of a flirt. And I'm not judging at all by this next observation, but I'm aware of your reputation, yet you don't seem like the type who needs a guy's attention to stroke your self-esteem."

Her expression is tight as she takes in everything I've just said. She reaches to her glass and takes a sip without breaking her stare. She finishes her drink, but holds the glass against her lips while she thinks. She eventually lowers it back to the table and looks down at her plate, picking up her fork.

"I'm not like that anymore," she says softly, avoiding my gaze.

"Like what?" I hate the sadness in her voice now. Why do I always say stupid shit?

"I'm not how I used to be."

Way to go, Daniel. Dumbass.

"Well, I didn't know you back then, so all I can do is judge the girl sitting in front of me right now. And so far, she's been a pretty damn cool date."

The smile spreads back to her lips. "That's good," she says, looking back up at me. "I wasn't sure what type of date I'd be, considering this is the first one I've ever been on."

"No need to stroke my ego," I say. "I can handle the fact that I'm not the first guy to ever express an interest in you."

"I'm serious," she says. "I've never been on a real date before. Guys tend to skip this whole part with me so they can just get to what they really want me for."

My smile disappears. I can tell by the look on her face she's being completely serious. I lean forward and look her hard in the eyes. "Those guys were all fucktards."

She laughs, but I don't.

"I'm serious, Six. Those guys all need a good kick to the clit, because dinner talk is by far the best part of you."

When the sentence leaves my mouth, the smile leaves her face. She looks at me like no one's ever given her a genuine compliment before. It pisses me off.

"How do you know this is the best part of me?" she asks, somehow finding that teasing, flirtatious tone in her voice again. "You haven't had the pleasure of kissing me yet. I'm pretty sure that's the best part of me, because I'm a phenomenal kisser."

Jesus Christ. I don't know if that was an invitation, but I want to send her my RSVP right this second. "I have no doubt being kissed by you would be fantastic, but if I had to choose, I'd take dinner talk over a kiss any day."

She narrows her eyes. "I call bullshit," she says with a challenging glare. "There's no way any guy would pick dinner talk over a good make-out session."

I attempt to return her challenging look, but she makes a good point.

"Okay," I admit. "Maybe you're right. But if I had my way, I'd pick kissing you *during* dinner talk. Get the best of both worlds."

She nods her head, impressed. "You're good," she says, leaning back in her seat. She folds her arms over her chest. "Where'd you learn those smooth moves?"

I wipe my mouth with my napkin, then set it on top of my plate. I lift my elbows until they're resting on the back of the booth and I smile at her. "I don't have smooth moves. I'm just charismatic, remember?"

Her mouth curls up into a grin and she shakes her head like she knows she's in trouble. Her eyes are smiling at me and I realize I've never felt like this before with any other girl. Not that I have it in my head that we're about to fall in love or we're soulmates or some shit like that. I've just never been around a girl where being myself was actually a good thing. With Val, I was always trying my hardest not to piss her off. With past girlfriends, I always found myself holding back from all the shit I really wanted to say. I've always felt like being myself with a girl wasn't necessarily a positive, because I'll be the first to admit, I can be a little over the top.

It's different with Six, though. Not only does she get my sense of humor and my personality, but I feel like she encourages it. I feel like the real me is what she likes the most and every time she laughs or smiles at the perfect moment, I want to fist bump her.

"You're staring at me," she says, breaking me out of my thoughts.

"So I am," I say, not bothering to look away.

She stares right back at me, but her demeanor and expression grow competitive as she narrows her eyes and leans forward. She's silently challenging me to a staring contest.

"No blinking," she says, confirming my thoughts.

"Or laughing," I say.

And it's on. We silently stare at each other for so long, my eyes begin to water and my grip tightens on the table. I try my hardest to keep my eyes locked on hers but they want to stare at every inch of her. I want to stare at her mouth and those full, pink lips and that soft, silky blonde hair. Not to mention her smile. I could stare at her smile all day.

In fact, I'm staring at it right now so I'm pretty sure that means I just lost the staring contest.

"I win," she says, right before she takes another drink of her water.

"I want to kiss you," I say bluntly. I'm a little shocked I said it, but not really. I'm pretty impatient and I really want to kiss her and I usually say whatever I'm thinking, so . . .

"Right now?" she asks, looking at me like I'm insane. She sets her glass back down on the table.

I nod. "Yep. Right now. I want to kiss you over dinner talk so I can have the best of both worlds."

"But I just ate onions," she says.

"So did I."

She's working her jaw back and forth, actually contemplating an answer. "Okay," she says with a shrug. "Why not?"

As soon as she gives me permission, I glance down at the table between us, wondering what the best way to do this would be. I could go sit with her on her side of the booth, but that might be invading her personal space too much. I reach in front of me and push my glass out of the way, then scoot hers to the left.

"Come here," I say, placing my hands on top of the table as I lean toward her. She must have thought I was kidding by the way her eyes dart nervously around us, taking in the fact that we're about to experience our first kiss in public.

"Daniel, this is awkward," she says. "Do you really want our first kiss to be in the middle of a restaurant?"

I nod. "So what if it's awkward? We'll have a do-over later. People put way too much stock in first kisses, anyway."

She tentatively places her palms facedown on the table, then pushes herself up and slowly leans in toward me. "Okay, then," she says, following her words up with a sigh. "But it would be so much better if you waited until the end of our date when you walk me to my front door and it'll be dark and we could be really nervous and you could accidentally touch my boob. That's how first kisses are supposed to be."

I laugh at her comment. We still aren't close enough for me to kiss her yet, but we're getting there. I lean forward a little more, but her eyes leave mine and focus on the table behind me.

"Daniel, there's a woman in the booth behind you changing her baby's diaper on the table. You're about to kiss me and the last thing I'll see before your lips touch mine is a woman wiping her infant's ass."

"Six. Look at me." She brings her eyes back to mine and we're finally close enough that I could reach her mouth. "Ignore the diaper," I command. "And ignore the two men in the booth to our left who are swigging their beer and watching us like I'm about to bend you over this table."

Her eyes dart to the left, so I catch her chin in my hand and force her attention back to me. "Ignore it all. I want to kiss you and I want you to want me to kiss you and I don't really feel like waiting until I walk you to your porch tonight because I've never really wanted to kiss someone this much before."

Her eyes drop to my mouth and I watch as everything around us disappears from her field of vision. Her tongue slips out of her mouth and glides nervously across her lips before it disappears again. I slide my hand from her chin to the nape of her neck and I pull her forward until our lips meet.

And holy shit, do they meet. Our mouths meld together like they used to be in love and they're just now seeing each other for the first time in years. My stomach feels like it's in the middle of a damn rave and my brain is trying to remember how to do this. It's like I suddenly forgot how to kiss, even though it's only been a day since I broke up with Val. I'm pretty sure I kissed Val yesterday, but for some reason my brain is acting like this is all new and it's telling me I should be parting my lips or teasing her tongue, but the signals just aren't making it to my mouth yet. Or my mouth is just ignoring me because it's been paralyzed by the soft warmth pressed against it.

I don't know what it is, but I've never held a girl's lips between mine for this long without breathing or moving or taking the kiss as far as I can possibly take it.

I inhale, even though I haven't taken a breath in almost a minute. I loosen my grip on the back of Six's head and begin to slowly pull my lips from hers. I open my eyes and hers are still closed. Her lips haven't moved and she's taking in shallow, quiet breaths as I remain poised close to her face, watching her.

I don't know if she expected more of a kiss. I don't know if she's ever had a peck last more than a minute before. I don't know what she's thinking, but I love the look on her face.

"Don't open your eyes," I whisper, still staring at her. "Give me ten more seconds to stare, because you look absolutely beautiful right now."

She tucks her bottom lip in with her teeth to hide her smile, but she doesn't move. My hand is still on the back of her head and I'm silently counting down from ten when I hear the waitress pause at our table.

"Y'all ready for your ticket?"

I hold up a finger, asking the waitress to give me a second. Well, five seconds to be exact. Six never moves a muscle, even after hearing the waitress speak. I count down silently until my ten seconds are up, then Six slowly opens her eyes and looks up at me.

I back away from her, putting several inches of space between us. I keep my eyes locked with hers. "Yes, please," I say, giving the waitress her answer. I hear her tear off the ticket and slap it down on the table. Six smiles, then begins laughing. She backs away from me and falls back down in her booth.

I breathe and it feels like the air is all brand new.

I slowly take my seat in the booth again, watching her laugh. She scoots the ticket toward me. "Your treat," she says.

I reach into my pocket and pull out my wallet, then lay cash down on top of the ticket. I stand up and reach out for Six's hand. She looks at it and smiles, then takes it. When she stands, I wrap my arm around her shoulder and pull her against me.

"Are you going to tell me how awesome that kiss was or are you going to ignore it?"

She shakes her head and laughs at me. "That wasn't even a real kiss," she says. "You didn't even try to put your tongue in my mouth."

I push open the doors to walk outside, but step aside and let her out first.

"I didn't have to put my tongue in your mouth," I say. "My kisses are that intense. I don't even really have to do anything. The only reason I pulled back was that I was sure we were about to experience a classic 'When Harry met Sally' moment."

She laughs again.

God, I love that she thinks I'm funny.

I open the passenger door for her and she pauses before climbing inside. She looks up at me. "You realize that classic scene is Sally proving a point about how easy it is for women to fake orgasms, right?"

God, I love that I think she's funny.

"Do I have to take you home yet?" I ask.

"Depends on what you have in mind next."

"Nothing really," I admit. "I just don't want to take you home yet. We could go to the park next to my house. They have a jungle gym."

She grins. "Let's do it," she says, holding up a tight fist in front of her.

I naturally bring my fist up and bump hers. She hops into the car and I shut her door, dumbfounded over the fact that she just fist bumped me.

The girl just fist bumped me and it was probably the hottest thing I've ever seen.

I walk to my side of the car and open the door, then take a seat. Before I crank the car I turn to look at her. "Are you really a guy?"

She raises an eyebrow, then pulls the collar of her shirt out and takes a quick glance down at her chest. "Nope. Pretty damn girl," she says.

"Are you dating someone?"

She shakes her head.

"Are you leaving the country tomorrow?"

"Nope," she says, her face obviously confused by my line of questions.

"What's your deal, then?"

"What do you mean?"

"Everyone has something and I can't figure yours out. You know, that one thing about themselves that's eventually a deal-breaker." I crank the car and begin to back out. "I want to know what yours is right now. My heart can't take another second of these tiny little things you do that drive me completely insane."

Her smile changes. It grows from a genuine smile to a guarded one. "We all have deal breakers, Daniel. Some of us just hope we can keep them hidden forever."

She rolls down her window again and the noise makes it impossible to continue the conversation. I'm almost positive the overwhelming scent of perfume is gone, so I'm curious if her need for the noise is why she rolled down the window this time.

• • •

"Do you bring all your dates here?" she asks.

I think about her question for a minute before answering. "Pretty much," I finally say after silently tallying the ends of all my dates. "I did take this chick out once in eleventh grade, but I took her home during the middle of the date because she got a stomach virus. I think she's the only one I never brought here."

She digs her heels into the dirt and comes to a stop in the swing. I'm standing behind her, so she turns around and looks up at me. "Seriously? You've brought all but one girl here?"

I shrug. Then nod. "Yeah. But none of them has ever wanted to literally *play* before. We usually just make out."

We've been here half an hour and already she's made me watch her on the monkey bars, push her on the merry-go-round and now I've been pushing her while she's been swinging for the last ten minutes. I'm not complaining, though. It's nice. Really nice.

"Have you ever had sex out here?" she asks.

I'm not sure how to take her bluntness. I've never really met anyone who asks the same straightforward questions I would, so I'm beginning to feel a little sympathetic to the people I put on the spot like this. I glance around the park until I see the makeshift wooden castle. I point to it. "You see the castle?"

She turns her head to look at the castle. "You had sex in there?"

I drop my arm and slide both my hands into the back pockets of my jeans. "Yep."

She stands and begins to walk in that direction.

"What are you doing?" I ask her. I'm not sure why she's heading toward the castle, but I'm almost positive it's not because she's weird and wants to have sex in the same spot I had sex with Val two weeks ago.

Does she?

God I hope not.

"I want to see where you had sex," she says, matter-of-fact. "Come show me."

This girl confuses the hell out of me. What's strange is how much I freaking love it. I begin jogging until I catch up with her. We walk until we reach the castle. She looks at me expectantly, so I point to the doorway. "Right in there," I say.

She walks to the doorway and peeks inside. She looks around for a minute, then pulls back out. "Looks really uncomfortable," she says.

"It was."

She smiles. "If I tell you something will you promise not to judge me?"

I roll my eyes. "It's human nature to judge."

She inhales a breath, then releases it. "I've had sex with six different people."

"At once?" I say.

She shoves my arm. "Stop. I'm trying to be honest with you here. I'm only eighteen and I lost my virginity when I was sixteen. Plus, I haven't had sex in about a year, so if you add it up, that's six people in just a little over fifteen months. That's like a whole new person every two and a half months. Only sluts do that."

"Why have you not had sex in over a year?"

She rolls her eyes and begins to walk past me. I follow her. When she reaches the swings, she takes her seat again. I sit in the swing beside her and twist my body until I'm facing her, but she faces forward.

"Why have you not had sex in over a year?" I say again. "You didn't like any of the boys you met in Italy?"

I can't see her face, but her body language reveals that this could be that *one thing*. The thing that changes it all for me.

"There was this one boy in Italy," she says softly. "But I don't want to talk about him. And yes, he's why I haven't had sex in over a year." She looks back at me. "Look, I know my reputation precedes me and I don't know if that's why you brought me here or what you expect to happen at the end of this date, but I'm not that girl anymore."

I lift my legs until my swing spins forward again. "The only thing I was hoping for at the end of this date was a kiss on your front porch," I say. "And maybe an accidental boob grab."

She doesn't laugh. I suddenly hate that I brought her here.

"Six, I didn't bring you here expecting anything. Yes, I've brought girls here in the past but that's only because I live across the street and I come here a lot. And yes, maybe I brought all those other girls here to have a little privacy while we made out, but that's only because I more than likely just wanted them to shut up and kiss me because they were getting on my everlasting nerves. But I only brought you here because I wasn't ready to take you home yet. I don't even really want to make out with you because I like talking to you too much."

I close my eyes, wishing I hadn't just said all that. I know girls like guys who play the uninterested asshole part. I'm usually pretty good at playing that part, but not with Six. Maybe because I usually am an uninterested asshole, but with her I'm as interested and curious and hopeful as I can possibly be.

"Which house is yours?" she asks.

I point across the street. "That one," I say, pointing to the one with the living room light on.

"Really?" she asks, sounding genuinely interested. "Is your family home?"

I nod. "Yeah, but you aren't meeting them. They're evil liars and I already told them I was never bringing you home to meet them."

I can feel her turn and look at me. "You told them you were never bringing me to meet them? So you already mentioned me?"

I meet her gaze. "Yes. I might have mentioned you."

She smiles. "Which one is your bedroom?"

"First window on the left side of the house. Chunk's bedroom is the window on the right. The one with the light on."

She stands up again. "Is your window unlocked? I want to see what your bedroom looks like."

Jesus, she's nosey.

"I don't want you to see my bedroom. I'm unprepared. It's messy."

She begins walking toward the street. "I'm going anyway."

I lean my head back and groan, then stand up and follow her toward the house.

"You're a piece of work," I say as we reach my window. She presses her palms against the glass and pushes up. The window doesn't budge, so I push her aside and open it for her. "I've never snuck into my own bedroom before," I admit. "I've snuck *out* before, but never in."

She begins to lift herself up over the ledge, so I grab her by the waist and assist her. She throws her leg over the edge of it and slips inside. I climb in behind her, then walk to the dresser and turn on my lamp. I make a scan of the room to ensure there isn't anything I don't want her to see. I kick a pair of underwear under the bed.

"I saw those," she whispers. She walks to my bed and presses her palms into the mattress, then straightens back up. She scans the room slowly, taking in everything about me. It feels weird, like I'm being exposed.

"I like your room," she says.

"It's a room."

She disagrees with a shake of her head. "No, it's more than that. This is where you live. This is where you sleep. This is where you feel the most privacy in your whole entire life. This is more than just a room."

"It doesn't feel very private right now," I say, watching as she skims her hand across every surface of my room. She turns and looks at me, then faces me full-on.

"What's the one thing in this room that tells the biggest secret about you?"

"I'm not telling you that."

She tilts her head. "So I'm right. You have secrets."

"I never said I didn't."

"Give me one," she asks. "Just one."

I'll give them all to her if she keeps looking at me like this. She's so damn adorable. I walk slowly toward her and she swallows a gulp of air. I stop when I'm several inches from her, then I nod my head down toward my mattress. "I've never kissed a girl on this bed," I whisper.

She looks down at my mattress, then back up to me. "I hope you really don't expect me to believe you've never made out with a girl in your room before."

"I didn't say that. I stated I had never kissed a girl on this particular bed. I was being honest, because it's a brand-new mattress. I just got it last week."

I can see the change in her eyes. The heavy rise and fall of her chest. She likes that I'm so close to her and she likes that I'm insinuating I want to kiss her on my bed.

Her eyes fall to the bed. "Are you saying you want to kiss me on your bed?"

I lean in closer until my lips are right next to her ear. "Are you saying you would let me?"

She sucks in a soft rush of air and I love that we're both feeling this. I want to kiss her on my bed so damn bad. I want it more than I even wanted the damn bed. Hell, I don't even care if it's on the bed. I just want to kiss her. I don't care where it is. I'll kiss her anywhere she'll allow me to kiss her.

I close the small gap between our bodies by resting my hands on her hips and pulling her to me. Her hands fly up to my forearms and she gasps. I dig my fingers into her hips and rest my cheek against hers. My mouth is still grazing her ear as I close my eyes, enjoying the feel of this.

I love the way she smells. I love the way she feels. And even though I haven't really given her an honest to God kiss yet, I already love the way she kisses.

"Daniel," she whispers. My name crashes against my shoulder when it rushes out of her mouth. "Will you take me home now?"

I wince at her words, immediately wondering what I just did wrong. I remain still for several long seconds, waiting until the feel of her against me no longer has me completely paralyzed.

"You didn't do anything wrong," she says, immediately easing the doubt building inside me. "I just think I should go home."

Her voice is soft and sweet and I suddenly hate every single guy in her past who has ever failed to get to know this side of her.

I don't release her immediately. I turn my head slightly until my forehead is touching the side of her head. "Did you love him?" I ask, allowing my brilliant brain to completely ruin this moment between us.

"Who?"

"The guy in Italy," I clarify. "The one who hurt you. Did you love him?"

Her forehead meets my shoulder and the way she fails to respond to that question reveals her answer, but it also fills me with so many more questions. I want to ask her if she still loves him. If she's still with him. If they still talk.

I don't say anything, though, because I have a feeling she wouldn't be here with me right now if any of that were the case. I bring my hand up to the back of her head and I press my lips into her hair. "Let's get you home," I whisper.

• • •

"Thanks for buying me dinner," she says when we reach her front door.

"You didn't really give me a choice. You left your house without a penny and then you shoved the bill in my face."

She laughs as she unlocks her front door, but doesn't open it yet. She turns back around and lifts her eyes, looking at me through lashes so long and thick, I have to refrain from reaching out and touching them.

Kissing her at dinner was definitely spontaneous, but I was sure it would make this moment a breeze.

It isn't.

If anything, I feel even more pressure to kiss her because it's already happened once tonight. And the fact that it's already happened and I know how damn good it feels makes me want it even more, but now I'm scared I've built it up too much.

I begin to lean in toward her when her lips part.

"Are you gonna use tongue this time?" she whispers.

I squeeze my eyes shut and take a step back, completely thrown off by her comment. I rub my palms down my face and groan.

"Dammit, Six. I was already feeling inadequate. Now you've just put expectations on it."

She's smiling when I look at her again. "Oh, there are definitely expectations," she says teasingly. "I expect this to be the most mind-blowing thing I've ever experienced, so you better deliver."

I sigh, wondering if the moment can possibly be recovered. I doubt it. "I'm not kissing you now."

She nods her head. "Yes you are."

I fold my arms over my chest. "No. I'm not. You just gave me performance anxiety."

She takes a step toward me and slides her hands between my folded arms, pushing against them until they unlock. "Daniel Wesley, you owe me a do-over since you made me kiss you in a crowded restaurant next to a dirty diaper."

"It wasn't crowded," I interject.

She glares at me. "Put your hands on my face and push me against this wall and slip me some tongue! Now!"

Before she can laugh at herself, my hands are casing her face and her back is pressed against the wall of her house and my lips are on hers. It happens so fast, it catches her off guard and she gasps, which causes her lips to part farther than she probably meant for them to. As soon as I caress the tip of her tongue with mine, she's clenching my shirt in two tight fists, pulling me closer. I tilt my head and take the kiss deeper, wanting to give her all the feels she can possibly get from a kiss and I want her to have them all at once.

My mouth isn't having a problem remembering what to do this time. What it's having a problem with is remembering how to slow down. Her hands are now in my hair and if she moans into my damn mouth one more time I'm afraid I might carry her to the backseat of my car and try to cheapen this date.

I can't do that. I can't, I can't, I can't. I like this girl too much already and I'll be damned if this isn't our first date and she already has me thinking about the next one. I brace my hands on the wall behind her head and I force myself to push off of her.

We're both panting. Gasping for breath. I'm breathing heavier than any kiss has ever made me breathe before. Her eyes are closed and I absolutely love how she doesn't immediately open them when I'm finished kissing her. I like that she seems to want to savor the way I make her feel, just like I want to savor her.

"Daniel," she whispers.

I groan and drop my forehead to hers, touching her cheek with my hand. "You make me love my name so damn much."

She opens her eyes and I pull back, looking down on her, still stroking her cheek. She's looking at me the same way I'm looking at her. Like we can't believe our luck.

"You better not turn out to be an asshole," she says quietly.

"And you better be done with that guy in Italy," I reply.

She nods. "I am," she says, although her eyes seem to tell a different story. I try not to read into it because whatever it is, it doesn't matter now. She's here with me. And she's happy about that. I can tell.

"You better not take back the girl who broke your heart last night," she adds.

I shake my head. "Never. Not after this. Not after you."

She seems relieved by my answer.

"This is scary," she whispers. "I've never had a boyfriend before. I don't know how this works. Do people become exclusive this fast? Are we supposed to pretend we're not that interested for a few more dates?"

Oh, dear God.

I've never been turned on by a girl laying claim to me before. I usually run in the other direction. She's obliterating every single thing I thought I knew about myself with every new sentence that passes those lips.

"I have no interest in faking disinterest," I say. "If you want to call yourself my girlfriend half as much as I wish you would, then it would save me a whole lot of begging. Because I was literally about to drop to my knees and beg you."

She squints her eyes playfully. "No begging. It screams desperation."

"You make me desperate," I say, pressing my lips to hers again. I choose to keep this kiss simple, even though I want to grab her face again and hold her against the wall. I pull away from her and we stare at each other. We stare at each other for so long I begin to worry that she's put some kind of spell on me, because I've never wanted to just stare at a girl like I want to stare at her. Just looking at her causes my heart to burn and my chest to constrict and I'm sort of freaking out that I barely know her at all and we've just made ourselves exclusive.

"Are you a witch?" I ask.

Her laugh returns and I suddenly don't care if she's a witch. If this is some kind of spell she's put on me, I hope it never breaks.

"I have no idea who you even are and now you're my damn girlfriend. What the hell have you done to me?"

She holds her palms up defensively. "Hey, don't blame me. I've gone eighteen years swearing off boyfriends and then you show up out of the blue with your vulgar mouth and terribly awkward first kisses and now look at me. I'm a hypocrite."

"I don't even know your phone number," I say.

"I don't even know your birthday," she says.

"You're the worst girlfriend I've ever had."

She laughs and I kiss her again. I notice I have to kiss her every time she laughs and she laughs a lot. Which means I have to kiss her a lot. God, I hope she doesn't laugh in front of Sky or Holder, because it's going to be so damn hard not to kiss her.

"You better not tell Sky about us," I say. "I don't want Holder to know yet."

"What about school? I enroll tomorrow. You don't think it'll be obvious when we interact?"

"We'll pretend we hate each other. It could be fun."

She tilts her face up and finds my mouth again, giving me a light peck. "But how do you plan on keeping your hands off me?"

I slide my other hand to her waist. "I won't keep my hands off you. I'll just touch you when they aren't looking."

"This is gonna be so much fun," she whispers.

I smile and pull her against me again. "Damn right it is." I dip my head and kiss her one last time. I release her, then reach behind her and turn the doorknob, pushing open her front door. "See you tomorrow."

She backs up two steps until she's in her doorway. "See you tomorrow."

She begins to turn and head into her house, but I grab her wrist and pull her back out. I wrap an arm around her lower back and lean in until my lips touch hers. "I forgot to accidentally touch your boob."

I catch her laugh with my mouth and graze her breast with the palm of my hand, then I immediately pull away from her. "Oops. Sorry."

She's covering her laugh with her hand as she backs into her house. She closes the door and I immediately fall to my knees, then onto my back. I stare straight up at the roof of her porch, wondering what in the hell just happened to my heart.

The door slowly reopens and she looks down at me, sprawled across her front porch like an idiot.

"I just needed a minute to recover," I say, smiling up at her. I'm not even excusing the fact that I'm shamelessly affected by her. She winks, then begins to close the door.

"Six, wait," I say, pushing myself up. She opens the door again and I reach up and grab the doorframe, then lean in toward her. "I know I just broke up with someone last night, but I need you to know you aren't a rebound. You know that, right?"

She nods. "I know," she says confidently. "Neither are you."

With that, she steps back into her house and closes her door.

Christ.

Motherfucking angel.

Chapter Three

"Let's go!" I tell Chunk for the fifth time.

She grabs her backpack and groans, then stands up and pushes her chair in. "What's your freakin' deal, Daniel? You're never in a hurry to get to school." She downs the rest of her orange juice. I'm standing at the door where I've been standing for five minutes, ready to leave. I hold open the front door and follow her outside.

Once we're in the car I don't even wait for her to shut her door before I'm putting it in reverse.

"Seriously, why are you in such a hurry?" she asks.

"I'm not in a hurry," I say defensively. "You were just being really slow."

The last thing she needs to know is how utterly pathetic I am. So pathetic I've been awake for two hours now, waiting until we could leave. I probably won't even see Six until lunch if we don't have classes together, so I really don't know why I'm in a hurry.

I didn't think about that. I hope we *do* have classes together.

"How was your date last night?" Chunk asks as she puts on her seatbelt.

"Good," I say.

"Did you kiss her?"

"Yep."

"Do you like her?"

"Yep."

"What's her name?"

"Six."

"No, really. What's her name?"

"*Six.*"

"No, not whatever nickname you gave her. What does everyone else call her?"

I roll my head and look at her. "Six. They call her Six."

Chunk scrunches up her nose. "Weird."

"It fits her."

"Do you love her?"

"Nope."

"Do you want to?"

"Ye—"

Whoa.

Hold up.

Do I want to?

I don't know. Maybe. Yes? Shit. I don't know. How screwed up is it that I broke up with a girl two days ago and I'm already contemplating the possibility of loving someone else?

Well, technically, I don't think I really loved Val. I sort of thought I did on occasion, but I think if a person is really, truly in love then it has to be unconditional. How I felt about Val was definitely not unconditional. I had conditions for every single feeling I had about her. Hell, the only reason I ever asked her out in the first place is that for about fifteen seconds, I thought she was Cinderella.

After that experience in the closet last year, that mystery girl was all I could think about. I looked for her everywhere, even though I had no idea what she looked like. I was pretty sure she had blonde hair, but it was dark, so I could have been wrong. I listened to every single girl's voice I walked past to see if they sounded like her. The problem was, they *all* sounded like her. It's hard to memorize a voice when you don't have a face to back it up with, so I would always find small things that reminded me of her in every girl I spoke to.

With Val, I actually convinced myself she was Cinderella. I was walking past her in the hallway one afternoon on my way to history class. I'd seen her in the past but never paid much attention because she seemed a little high-maintenance for me. I accidentally bumped her shoulder when I passed her because my head was turned and I was talking to someone else. She called out after me, "Watch it, kid."

I froze in my tracks. I was too scared to turn around because hearing her use the term "kid" had me convinced I was about to come face to face with the girl from the closet. When I finally gained the courage to turn around, I was floored by how hot she was. I always hoped if I ever found out who Cinderella was that I'd be attracted to her. But Val was way hotter than how I'd been fantasizing.

I walked back up to her and made her repeat what she said. She looked shocked, but she repeated it anyway. When the words fell from her mouth again, I immediately leaned forward and kissed her. As soon as I kissed her I knew she wasn't Cinderella. Her mouth was different. Not *bad* different, just different. When I pulled back after realizing it wasn't her, I was a little annoyed with myself for not just letting it go. I was never going to find out who the girl was, so there was no point in dwelling on it. Plus, Val really was hot. I forced myself to ask her out that day and thus began "the relationship."

"You just passed my school," Chunk says.

I slam on the brakes when I realize she's right. I kick the car into reverse and back up, then pull over to let her out. She looks out the passenger window and sighs.

"Daniel, we're so early there isn't even anyone else here yet."

I lean forward and look out her window, scanning the school. "Not true," I say, pointing to someone pulling into a parking spot. "There's someone."

She shakes her head. "That's the maintenance guy. I beat the freaking maintenance guy to school." She opens her door and steps out, then turns and leans into the car before shutting her door. "Do I need to plan for you to be here to pick me up an hour early, too? Is your brain stuck in eastern time today?"

I ignore her comment and she shuts the door, then I hit the gas and drive toward my school.

• • •

I don't know what kind of car she drives, so I pull into my usual spot and wait. There are a few other cars here, including Sky and Holder's, but I know they're at the track running like they do every morning.

I can't believe I don't know what kind of car she drives. I also still don't know her phone number. Or her birthday. Or her favorite color or what she wants to be when she's older or why the hell she chose Italy for her foreign exchange or what her parents' names are or what kind of food she eats.

My palms begin to sweat, so I wipe them on my jeans, then grip my steering wheel. What if she's really annoying around other people? What if she's a junkie? What if . . .

"Hey."

Her voice breaks me out of my near–panic attack. It also calms me the hell down because as soon as I see her sliding into the front seat of my car, my unjustified fears are replaced by pure relief.

"Hey."

She shuts her door and pulls her leg up, turning to face me in the car. She smells so good. She doesn't smell like perfume at all. She just smells good. Kind of fruity.

"Have you had your panic attack yet?" she asks.

Confusion clouds my face. I don't have time to answer her before she begins talking again.

"I had one this morning," she says, looking at everything else around us, unable to make eye contact with me. "I just keep thinking we're idiots. Like maybe this connection we think we have is all in our heads and we didn't really have as much fun as we thought we did last night. I don't even know you, Daniel. I don't know your birthday, your middle name, Chunk's real name, if you have any pets, what your major will be in college. I know it's not like we made this huge commitment or got married or had sex, but you have to understand that I have never thought the idea of having a boyfriend was even remotely appealing and maybe I still don't think it's all that appealing, but . . ."

She finally looks at me and makes eye contact. "But you're so funny and this entire past year has been the worst year of my life and for some reason when I'm with you it feels good. Even though I hardly know you, the parts of you I do know I really, really like." She leans her head into the headrest and sighs. "And you're cute. Really cute. I like staring at you."

I turn in my seat and mirror her position by resting my head against my own headrest. "Are you finished?"

She nods.

"I had my panic attack right before you got in the car just now. But when you opened your door and I heard your voice, it went away. I think I'm good now."

She smiles. "That's good."

I smile back at her and we both just stare at each other for several seconds. I want to kiss her, but I also kind of like just staring at her. I would hold her hand, but she's running her fingers up and down the seam of the passenger seat and I like watching her do that.

"I should go inside and register for classes now," she says.

"Make sure you get second lunch."

She nods. "I can't wait to pretend I hate you today."

"I can't wait to pretend I hate you more."

I can tell she's about to turn, so I lean forward and slip my hand behind her neck, then pull her to me. I kiss her good morning, hello and good-bye all at once. When I pull back, I glance over her shoulder and see Sky and Holder making their way off the track and toward the parking lot.

"Shit!" I push her head down between us. "They're coming this way."

"Crap," she whispers.

She begins humming the theme to *Mission Impossible* and I start laughing. I start to crouch down with her, but if they reach my car they'll see us whether our heads are down or not.

"I'll get out of the car so they don't come over here."

"Good idea," she says, her voice muffled by her arms. "I think you just gave me whiplash."

I lean over and kiss the back of her head. "Sorry. I'll see you later. Lock my doors when you get out."

I open the car door just as Holder begins to head in my direction. I start walking their way to intercept them. "Good run?" I ask when I reach them.

They both nod, out of breath. "I need my change of clothes," Sky says to Holder, pointing to her car. "Want me to grab yours?" Holder nods and she heads in that direction. Holder's eyes move from hers over to mine.

"Why are you here so early?" he asks. He doesn't ask it like he's accusing me of anything. He's probably just making small talk, but I already feel defensive.

"Chunk had to be at school early," I say.

He nods and grabs the hem of his shirt, then wipes sweat off his forehead. "You still coming tonight?"

I think about his question. I think really hard, but I'm drawing a blank about what could be going on tonight that I would need to go to.

"Daniel, do you even know what the hell I'm talking about?"

I shake my head. "No idea," I admit.

"Dinner at Sky's house. Karen invited you and Val? They're having a big welcome-back thing for Sky's best friend."

That gets my attention. "Yeah, of course I'll be there. Not bringing Val, though. We broke up, remember?"

"Yeah, but dinner is still ten hours away. You might love her again by then."

Sky walks up and hands Holder his bag. "Daniel, have you seen Six?"

"No," I immediately blurt out.

Sky glances toward the school, not having noticed the defensiveness in my immediate response. "She must be registering for classes inside." She turns to Holder. "I'm gonna go find her." She reaches up and kisses him on the cheek, but Holder's eyes remain on mine.

They're narrowed.

This isn't good.

Sky walks away and I begin to walk right behind her, toward the school. Holder's hand lands on my shoulder when I pass him, so I pause. I turn around, but it takes me a few seconds to look him in the eyes. When I do, he doesn't look happy.

"Daniel?"

I raise an eyebrow to match his expression. "Holder?"

"What are you up to?"

"I do not know what you are talking about," I reply innocently.

"You do know what I am talking about because when you are lying, you do not use contractions when you speak."

I ponder his observation for a few seconds. *Is that true?*

Shit. It's true.

I breathe out a heavy breath and do my best to look like I'm giving him a confession. "Fine," I say, kicking at the dirt beneath my feet. "I had sex with Val just now. In my car. I didn't want you to know because you and Sky seemed excited that we broke up."

Tension releases from Holder's shoulders and he shakes his head. "Dude, I could care less who you date. You know that." He begins walking toward the school, so I follow suit. "Unless it's Six," he adds. "You aren't allowed to date Six."

I keep walking forward, even though that comment makes me want to freeze. "I have no desire to date Six," I say. "She's not really that cute, anyway."

He stops in his tracks and spins around to face me. He holds up a finger like he's about to lecture me. "You're not allowed to talk shit about her, either."

Christ. Hiding our relationship from him may be more exhausting than it is fun. "No loving her, no hating her, no screwing her, no dating her. Got it. Anything else you want to add?"

He thinks for a second, then lowers his arm. "Nope. That covers it. See you at lunch." He turns and walks inside. I glance back to the parking lot in time to see Six sneaking out of my car. She gives me a quick wave. I wave back, then turn and head inside.

●　　●　　●

I walk my tray toward the table and internally rejoice when I see the only available spot is right next to Six. She glances at me as I walk up and her eyes smile, but only briefly. I set my tray down across from Holder and find my way into the current conversation. Everyone is discussing the dinner at Sky's house tonight, but I've had dinner there before. Karen doesn't know what real food is. She's vegan, so I normally turn down meals at their house. Not tonight, though.

"Will there be meat?" I ask.

Sky nods. "Yeah. Jack's actually cooking, so the food should be good. I also baked a chocolate cake."

I reach across the table for the salt, even though I don't need it. It gives me an excuse to lean in ridiculously close to Six.

"So, Six. How do you like your classes?" I ask casually.

She shrugs. "They're okay."

"Let me see your schedule."

She narrows her eyes like I'm doing something wrong. I give her a look to let her know she has nothing to worry about. Even if I wasn't into her, I'm not an asshole. I'd still be making conversation with her.

"It sucks we don't have any classes together," Sky says. "Who do you have for history?"

Six pulls her schedule out of her pocket and hands it to me. I open it and make a quick scan of the classes, but none are the same as mine. "Carson for history," I say, replying to Sky's question. I hand Six back her schedule and give her a look to let her know we don't have any classes together. She looks bummed, but says nothing.

"Can you speak Italian very well?" Breckin asks Six.

"Not well at all. I speak better Spanish than I do Italian. I chose Italy because I had enough funding and I'd rather have spent half a year there than in Mexico."

"Good choice," Breckin says. "The men are hotter in Italy."

Six nods. "Yes they are," she says appreciatively.

I immediately lose my appetite and drop my fork onto my plate. It makes a loud clanking noise, so naturally everyone turns to look at me. It's quiet and awkward and everyone is still staring, so I say the first thing on my mind. "Italian men are too hairy."

Sky and Breckin laugh, but Six purses her lips together and looks back down at her plate.

God, I suck at this.

Luckily, Val walks up and takes everyone's attention off me.

Wait. Did I just say luckily? Because Val walking up is *not* a good thing.

"Can I talk to you?" she says, glaring down at me.

"Do I have a choice?"

"Hallway," she says, spinning on her heels. She heads toward the exit to the cafeteria.

"Do us all a favor and go see what Val wants," Sky says. "If you don't meet her out there she'll come back to the table."

"*Please*," Breckin mutters.

I'm watching all their reactions and I don't know if they've always reacted this way when it comes to Val or if I'm only recognizing it for the first time because I finally have clarity.

"Why is everyone referring to Tessa Maynard as *Val?*" Six asks, confused.

Breckin points over his shoulder in the direction Val walked off in. "Tessa is Val. Val is Tessa. Daniel can't seem to call anyone by their actual name, if you haven't noticed."

I watch as Six inhales a slow breath, then looks directly at me. She looks really disgusted. "Your girlfriend is Tessa Maynard? You have sex with Tessa Maynard?"

"*Ex*-girlfriend and *had* sex," I clarify. "And yes. Probably coincided with the same time you were falling in love with a hairy Italian."

Six's eyes narrow, then she quickly looks away. I instantly feel bad for what I said, but I was only kidding. Sort of. We're *supposed* to be mean to each other. I can't tell if I really hurt her feelings or if she's just a really good actress.

I sigh, then stand up and head toward the cafeteria doors in a hurry so I can get back to the table and somehow make sure Six really isn't pissed at me.

I make it out to the hallway and Val is standing right outside the cafeteria doors. "I'll take you back under one condition," she says.

I'm curious what the condition is, but it doesn't really matter at this point.

"Not interested."

Her mouth literally drops open. It's not even that cute a mouth now that I'm looking at it. I don't know how I fell for it all those other times.

"I'm serious, Daniel," she says firmly. "If you screw up one more time, I'm done."

I let my head fall backward until I'm looking up at the ceiling. "Jesus, Tessa," I say. She's not really worthy of my nicknames anymore. I look her in the eyes again. "I don't want you to take me back. I don't want to date you. I don't even want to make out with you. You're mean."

She scoffs, but stands frozen. "Are you serious?" she says, dumbfounded.

"Serious. Positive. Convinced. Enlightened. Take your pick."

She throws her hands up in the air and spins around, then walks back into the cafeteria. I walk to the doors and open them. Six is staring at me from our table, so I make a quick glance around at the rest of the group. No one is paying attention, so I motion for her to come out into the hallway. She takes a quick drink of her water, then stands, making up an excuse to the rest of the table. I step out of view while she makes her way to the exit. When the doors open I immediately grab her by the wrist and pull her until we reach the lockers. I push her against them and crash my mouth to hers. Her hands immediately fly up to my hair and we rush our kisses like we might get caught.

And we really might.

After a good solid minute, she pushes lightly against my chest, so I pull away from her.

"Are you mad?" I ask her, almost blurting out the question between heavy breaths.

"No," she says, shaking her head. "Why would I be mad?"

"Because Val is Tessa and you obviously don't like Tessa very much and because I had a jealous moment and called Italian men hairy."

She laughs. "We're acting, Daniel. I was actually a little impressed. And kind of turned on when you got jealous. But highly *un*impressed with the fact that Val is Tessa. I can't believe you had sex with Tessa Maynard."

"I can't believe you had sex with pretty much everyone else," I reply teasingly.

She grins. "You're a jerk."

"You're a slut."

"Will you be at my dinner tonight?" she asks.

"That's a really dumb question."

A smile spreads slowly across her face and it's so damn sexy I have to kiss her again.

"I should get back," she whispers when I pull away.

"Yes, you should. So should I."

"You first. I'm supposed to be in the administration office clearing up an issue with my schedule."

"Okay," I say. "I'll go first, but I'll miss you until you get back to the table."

"Don't make me puke," she says.

"I bet you're adorable when you puke. I bet your actual puke is even adorable. It's probably bubble-gum pink."

"You're seriously disgusting." She laughs and reaches up to kiss me again. She pushes against my chest, then slips out from between me and the locker. She puts both of her hands on my back and pushes me toward the cafeteria doors. "Act natural."

I turn and wink at her, then walk back through the doors. I casually make my way back to the table and take a seat.

"Where's Six?" Breckin asks.

I shrug. "How should I know? I was busy making out with Val in the hallway."

Sky shakes her head and lays her fork down. "I just lost my appetite, Daniel. Thanks."

"You'll have your appetite back by dinner tonight," I say.

Sky shakes her head. "Not with you and Val there. You'll probably be sucking face next to my food. If you drool on my chocolate cake you aren't getting any."

"Sorry, Cheese Tits," I say. "But Val won't be at your dinner tonight. I'll be there, though."

"I bet you will," Breckin says under his breath.

I glance over at him and he looks at me challengingly.

"What'd you just mumble, Powder Puff?" He absolutely hates it when I call him Powder Puff, but he should know I only give nicknames to the people I like. I think he does know that, though, because he doesn't really give me too much shit about it.

"I said I bet you will," he repeats louder this time. He turns to Sky, who is seated right next to him. "Six, right?"

Sky nods. "Six or six-thirty."

"I'll be there at six," Breckin says. He looks back at me and smirks. "I bet you'll be there at six, too, right, Daniel? You like six? Is six good for you?"

He's on to us. Fucker.

"Six is perfect," I say, holding his stare. "My absolute favorite time of day."

He smiles knowingly, but I'm not worried. I have a feeling he's going to have just as much fun with this as I am.

"All cleared up?" Sky asks Six when she returns to the table. Six nods and takes her seat. Her hand brushes across my outer thigh when she adjusts herself. I press my knee against hers and we both pick our forks up at the same time and take a bite of food.

Having her here just inches from me and not being allowed to touch her is complete torture. I'm beginning to think I'd rather just lean over and kiss her and take Holder's ass beating than have to pretend I don't want her.

Since the moment she disappeared into her house last night I've felt more restless than I've ever felt before. I've been fidgeting all day. I can't stop tapping my fingers and shaking my leg. It feels like I want to scratch at my skin when she's not around, like I'm coming down from a high.

That's exactly what this feels like. Like she's a drug I've become immediately addicted to, but I have none in supply. The only thing that satiates the craving is her laugh. Or her smile or her kiss or the feel of her pressed against me.

God, it's so hard not to touch her. So hard.

She begins laughing loudly at something Sky said and the craving becomes almost intolerable because of the intense need I have to catch that sound with my mouth.

I drop my fork onto my plate and lower my head into my hands and groan. "Stop laughing," I say quietly.

She's obviously laughing too loud to hear me, so I turn toward her and say it again. "Six. Stop laughing. Please."

Her jaw clamps shut and she turns to look at me. "Excuse me?"

About that same time, Holder kicks the shit out of my knee. I scoot back and immediately pull my leg up and rub the spot he kicked. "What the hell, man?"

Holder looks at me like I'm clueless. "What the hell is wrong with you? I told you not to be mean to her."

Ha. He thinks I'm being mean? If he only knew how nice I want to be to her right now.

"You don't like my laugh?" Six says. I can tell in her voice she knows how much I like her laugh, but she's enjoying the fact that Holder is clueless to what her laugh does to me.

"No," I grumble, scooting back toward the table.

She laughs again and the sound of it causes me to wince.

"Are you always this grumpy?" she asks. "Do you want me to go get your girlfriend and bring her back to the table so she can put you in a better mood?"

"No!" Sky and Breckin yell in unison.

I look at Six. "You think my girlfriend could put me in a better mood?"

She grins. "I think your *girlfriend* is a pathetic idiot for agreeing to date you."

I shake my head. "My girlfriend makes incredibly wise decisions. I can't wait until tonight when I get to show her just how smart she was when she decided to lay claim to me."

"I thought you said she wasn't coming to dinner," Sky says, disappointed.

Six's hand slips under the table and she begins to gently rub at the spot on my knee that Holder just finished kicking.

"Jesus Christ," I mutter, leaning forward. I put my elbows on the table and run my hands up and down my face, attempting to appear unaffected by the fact that it feels like Six just crawled her way inside my chest and is wrapping herself around my heart.

"Is lunch over yet?" I say to no one in particular. "I need to get out of here."

Holder looks at his phone. "Five more minutes." He looks back up at me. "Are you sick, Daniel? You're not being yourself today. It's starting to freak me out a little bit."

Six's hand is still on my knee. I casually lower my hand and slide it under the table, then place it over hers. She flips her hand over and I lace our fingers together and squeeze her hand.

"I know," I say to Holder. "I'm just having a weird day. Girl-friends. They have that effect on you."

He's still looking at me suspiciously. "You seriously need to make up your mind when it comes to her. It's past the point that any of us feel sorry for you, because now it's just irritating."

"Doesn't help that she used to be a slut," Six says.

"Six!" Sky says with a laugh. "That was so mean."

Six shrugs. "It's true. Daniel's girlfriend used to be a big, fat slut. I heard she had sex with six different guys in just over a year."

"Don't talk about my girlfriend that way," I say. "Who gives a shit what she did in the past? I sure as hell don't."

Six squeezes my hand, then pulls hers away and brings her hand back up to the table. "Sorry," she says. "That wasn't nice. If it helps, I heard she's a good kisser."

I grin. "*Phenomenal* kisser."

The bell rings and everyone picks up their trays. I notice Six isn't in any hurry, so I take my time as well. Sky kisses Holder on the cheek, then walks off with Breckin toward the exit. Holder picks up both their trays and lifts his eyes to mine. "I'll see you tonight," he says. "And I hope to hell the real Daniel shows up, because you aren't making a whole lot of sense today."

"I know," I say, pointing briefly at my head. "She's got me all screwed up in here, man. All screwed up. I'm losing my mind."

Holder shakes his head. "That right there is exactly what I'm talking about. You seem more affected by Val today than you ever have. It's just weird." He walks off, still looking confused. I feel sort of bad for lying to him, but it's his own fault. He shouldn't try to tell me who I can date, then I wouldn't have to hide it from him.

"That was fun," Six says quietly. She begins to pick up her tray, but I intercept it. I take a step toward her and look her hard in the eyes.

"Don't you ever insult my girlfriend again. You hear me?"

She tightens her lips to hide her smile. "Noted."

"I want to walk you to your locker. Wait for me."

Her smile becomes harder for her to hide as she nods her head. I take both of our trays and place them on the tray pile, then walk back to the table. I glance around us and don't really see anyone paying attention, so I quickly lean in and kiss her briefly on the lips, then pull away.

"Daniel Wesley, you're gonna get caught," she says with a grin. She turns and begins walking toward the exit, so I discreetly place a hand on her lower back and walk next to her.

"God, I hope so," I say. "If I have to sit through another lunch like that, I'll lose my shit and you'll end up on your back on top of the table."

She laughs. "What a way with words you have."

We exit the cafeteria and I walk her to her locker. It's on the opposite hall from mine, which couldn't be more inconvenient. We don't have a single class together and I won't even see her in the hallway while we're at school. I know I haven't even been dating her for an entire day, but I already miss her.

"Can I come over before dinner?" I ask her.

She shakes her head. "No, I'll be helping Karen and Sky prep. I'm going over there right after school."

"What about after dinner?"

She shakes her head again while she switches her books. "Sky crawls through my window every night. You can't be in my room."

"I thought your window was out of commission."

"Only to people with penises."

I laugh. "What if I told you I didn't have a penis?"

She glances at me. "I would probably rejoice. My experiences with people who have penises never end well."

I shake my head. "That's not something my penis wants to hear you say. He has a very sensitive ego."

She smiles and shuts her locker, then leans against it. "Well, maybe you should go home after school and stroke his ego a little bit until he feels better."

I cock an eyebrow. "You just made a masturbation joke."

She nods. "So I did."

"I have the coolest girlfriend in the world."

She nods again. "So you do."

"I'll see you at dinner."

"So you will," she says.

"Can we sneak off and make out while everyone's eating?"

She squints her eyes as if she's actually contemplating it. "Don't know. We'll play it by ear."

I nod and lean my shoulder against the locker next to hers. We're just a few inches apart and we're staring at each other again. I love how she looks at me like she actually enjoys staring at me.

"Give me your phone number," I say.

"As long as you aren't planning to text me pics of your ego stroking after school."

I clutch at my heart. "Dammit, Six. I love every single word that comes out of your mouth."

"Cock," she says dryly.

She's evil.

"Except that word," I say. "I don't love cock."

She laughs and opens her locker again. She takes out a pen, then turns and grabs my hand. She writes her phone number down, then puts the pen back in her locker. "I'll see you tonight, Daniel." She begins backing away. All I can do is nod, because I'm pretty sure her voice just hardcore made out with my ears. She turns and disappears down the hallway just as something appears in my line of sight.

I look to the eyes that are now glaring at me.

"What do you want, Powder Puff?" I ask him, pushing off the locker.

"You like her?"

"Who?" I ask, playing dumb. I don't know why I'm trying to play dumb. We both know who he's referring to.

"I think it's adorable," he says. "She likes you, too. I can tell."

"Really?"

"You're too easy. And yes, I don't know how, but I can tell she likes you. Y'all are cute. Why are you hiding it? Or better yet, who are you hiding it from?"

"Holder. He says I can't date her." I begin walking toward class and Breckin falls into step with me.

"Why not? Because you're an asshole?"

I stop and look at him. "I'm an asshole?"

Breckin nods. "Yeah. I thought you knew that."

I laugh, then start walking again. "He thinks it'll screw everything up since we're all best friends."

"He's right. It will."

I stop walking again. "Who's to say things won't work out with me and Six?"

"Didn't you just meet her? Like two days ago?"

"Doesn't matter," I say defensively. "She's different. I have a good feeling about her."

Breckin studies me for a moment, then he smiles. "This should be fun. I'll see you tonight." He turns and walks in the opposite direction, but he stops and faces me again. "Call me Powder Puff again and your secret is out."

"Okay, Powder Puff."

He laughs and points at me. "See? Such an *ass*hole."

He spins and heads toward his class. I pull my phone out of my pocket and open up Val's contact information. I hit delete, then add Six's number into my phone. I'll wait until I make it to my classroom before I text her.

Don't want to seem desperate.

Chapter Four

Me: Pretend you're going to the bathroom or something.

I place my phone back down on the table and begin eating again. I've been here almost an hour and Six and I have barely had a chance to talk. I don't know if I'll even need Breckin to out us, because I'm about to lose my patience and do it myself.

I know everyone's curious about her trip to Italy, but she seems uncomfortable talking about it. Her answers are short and clipped and I hate that I'm the only one who seems to notice how much she doesn't want to bring up Italy. I also like that I'm the only one who notices, because it proves that whatever connection I feel with her is more than likely genuine. I feel like I know her better than anyone else here. Maybe even better than Sky knows her.

Although it's absurd to feel that way, since I still don't even know her birthday.

Six: There's only one bathroom in the hallway. Even if I were to go there it would be obvious if you got up and followed me.

I read her text and groan out loud.

"Everything okay?" Jack asks. He's seated next to me at the table, which is fine any other time but I really wanted Six to be in his chair. I nod, then put my phone facedown on the table.

"Irritating girlfriend drama," I say.

He nods and turns back to Holder, continuing with their conversation. Six is involved in a discussion with Sky and Karen. Breckin ended up not being able to come, which was probably a good thing. Not sure I could have handled the fact that he knows.

Right now it's just me and my impatience having a silent war at the dinner table.

"That reminds me," Six says loudly. "I bought you all presents. I forgot." She scoots back from the table. "They're at my house. I'll be right back." She stands and takes two steps before turning back toward us. "Daniel? They're kind of heavy. Mind giving me a hand?"

Don't act too excited, Daniel.

I sigh heavily. "I guess," I say as I scoot back from the table. I look at Holder and roll my eyes, then follow Six outside. Neither of us says a word while we make our way to the side of the house. She reaches her window, then turns around.

"I lied," she says. Her eyes are worried, which causes me to worry.

"About what?"

She shakes her head. "I didn't buy anyone presents. I just can't take another second of all the questions, and then seeing you across the table and knowing how much I just wish it could be the two of us is making this whole dinner really irritating. But now I don't have presents. How do I go back in there without presents?"

I try not to laugh, but I love that she's been just as irritated as I've been. I was starting to worry I might have a few issues.

"We could just stay out here and never go back inside."

"We could," she says in agreement. "But they'd eventually come look for us. Not to mention it would be rude, since Jack and Karen went through all this trouble to cook for me and oh, my God, what if it's true, Daniel?"

I don't know if it's me or if she's just really difficult to keep up with, but I have no idea what she's talking about. "What if what's true?"

She exhales a quick breath. "What if our feelings are just reverse psychology? What if Holder had told you to date me Saturday night? You might not have been interested in me after that. What if the only reason we like each other so much is that it's forbidden? What if the second they all find out the truth, we can't stand each other?"

I hate that the worry in her voice sounds genuine, because that means she actually believes the shit she's saying right now.

"You think there's a chance I only like you because I'm not supposed to like you?"

She nods.

I grab her hand and yank her back toward the front of the house.

"Daniel, I don't have presents!"

I ignore her and walk her up the front steps, open the door, and march her straight into the kitchen.

"Hey!" I yell. Everyone turns around and looks at us. I glance at Six and her eyes are wide. I inhale a deep breath, then turn back to the table. Specifically to Holder.

"She fist bumped me," I say, pointing at Six. "It's not my fault. She hates purses and she fist bumped me, then she made me push her on the damn merry-go-round. After that, she demanded to see where I had sex in the park, then she forced me to sneak into my own bedroom. She's weird and half the time I can't keep up with her, but she thinks I'm funny as hell. And Chunk asked me this morning if I wanted to love her someday, and I realized I've never hoped I could love someone more than I want to love her. So every single one of you who has an issue with us dating is going to have to get over it because . . ." I pause and turn toward Six. "Because you fist bumped me and I could care less who knows we're together. I'm not going anywhere and I don't want to go anywhere so stop thinking I'm into you because I'm not supposed to be into you." I lift my hands and tilt her face toward mine. "I'm into you because you're awesome. And because you let me accidentally touch your boob."

She's smiling wider than I've ever seen her smile. "Daniel Wesley, where'd you learn those smooth moves?"

"Not moves, Six. Charisma."

She throws her arms around my neck and kisses me. I wait for the moment Holder yanks me away from her, but that moment doesn't come. We kiss for a solid thirty seconds before people begin clearing their throats. When Six pulls away from me, she's still smiling.

"Does it feel different now that they know?" I ask her. "Because it actually feels better to me."

She shoves my chest. "Stop! Stop saying things that make me grin like an idiot. My face has been hurting since the second I met you."

I pull her to me and hug her, then suddenly become aware that we're still standing in Sky's kitchen and everyone is still staring at us. I hesitantly turn and look at Holder to gauge his level of anger. He's never actually hit me before, but I've seen what he can do and I sure as hell don't want to experience it.

When my eyes meet his, he's . . . smiling. He's actually smiling.

Sky has a napkin to her eyes and she's wiping tears away.

Karen and Jack are both smiling.

It's weird.

Too weird.

"Do you guys talk to my parents?" I ask cautiously. "Did they teach you their dirty reverse psychology tricks?"

Karen is the first to speak. "Sit down, you two. Your food is getting cold."

I kiss Six on the forehead, then take my seat back at the table. I keep glancing at Holder, but he doesn't look upset at all. He actually looks a little impressed.

"Where the hell is my present?" Jack asks Six.

She clears her throat. "I decided to wait until Christmas." She picks up her glass and brings it to her lips, then glances at me. I smile at her.

Everyone else resumes whatever conversations were going on before my interruption. It's like no one is even that shocked. They act like it's completely normal. Like it's a natural thing . . . me and Six.

And I totally get it, because it is. Whatever we have is good, and even though I still don't know her birthday, I know this is right. And based on the look on her face right now, so does she.

• • •

"I really like this one," I say, looking at the picture in my hands. I'm leaning against the wall, sitting on the floor in Sky's bedroom. Six is passing around pictures she took in Italy to Sky, Holder, and me.

"Which pic are you looking at?" she says. She's lying next to me on the floor. I look down at her and flip the photo over so she can see it. She shakes her head with a quick roll of her eyes. "You only like that one because my cleavage looks great."

I immediately turn the photo back around. She's right. It does look great. But that's not at all why I liked it at first. She looks happy in this one. Peaceful.

"I took that picture the day I got to Italy," she says. "You can keep it."

"Thank you. I wasn't planning on giving it back to you, anyway."

"Consider it an anniversary present," she says.

I immediately look down at the time on my phone. "Oh. Wow. It really is our anniversary." I readjust myself until I'm leaning over her. "I almost forgot. I'm the worst boyfriend ever. I can't believe you haven't dumped me yet."

She grins. "That's okay. You can remember the next one." She slips her hand to the back of my neck and pulls me forward until our lips meet.

"*Anniversary?*" Sky says, confused. "Exactly how long have the two of you been dating?"

I pull away from Six and sit back up against the wall. "Precisely twenty-four hours."

An awkward silence follows, then of course Holder fills it. "Am I the only one who has a bad feeling about this?"

"I think it's great," Sky says. "I've never seen Six so . . . nice? Happy? Spoken for? It's a good look for her."

Six sits up and wraps her arms around my neck, then pulls me to the floor with her. "That's because I've never met anyone as vulgar and inappropriate and horrible at first kisses as Daniel." She pulls my mouth to hers and kisses me while she laughs at herself.

This is a first. A kiss and a laugh at the same time? I think I might be in heaven.

"Six has a bedroom, too, you know," Holder says.

Six stops laughing. *And* she stops kissing me.

Holder is about to be put on my shit list.

"Six doesn't allow penises in her bedroom," I reply to him while still staring down at her.

Six moves her mouth to my ear. "As long as you don't expect me to stroke his ego tonight, I kind of want to kiss you on my bed."

I didn't know people could move as fast as I'm moving right now. This has to be some sort of record, because my hands are under her back and knees and I'm scooping her up in my arms before her sentence even completely registers. She throws her arms around my neck and squeals as I head straight for Sky's window. I put her down gently, but then practically shove her outside. I begin to follow right behind her without even telling Sky or Holder good-bye.

"They are so strange together," I hear Sky say right before I'm out the window.

"Yeah," Holder says in agreement. "But also oddly . . . *right.*"

I pause.

Did Holder just compliment my relationship with Six? I don't know why I always want his approval so much, but hearing him say that fills me with this weird sense of pride. I turn around and take a step back to the window and lean inside. "I heard that."

He looks at the window and sees me leaning inside, so he rolls his eyes. "Go away," he says with a laugh.

"No. We're having a moment."

He cocks an eyebrow, but doesn't respond.

"You're my best friend, Holder."

Sky shakes her head and laughs, but Holder is still looking at me like I've lost my mind.

"For real," I say. "You're my best friend and I love you. I'm not ashamed to admit that I love a guy. I love you, Holder. Daniel Wesley loves Dean Holder. Always and forever."

"Daniel, go make out with your girlfriend," he says, waving me off.

I shake my head. "Not until you tell me you love me, too."

His head falls back against Sky's headboard. "I fucking love you, now GO AWAY!"

I grin. "I love you more."

He picks up a pillow and tosses it at the window. "Get the hell out of here, dipshit. "

I smile and back away from the window.

"You two are so strange together," Sky says to him.

I pull the window shut, then turn around to find Six. She's already in her bedroom, leaning out her window with her chin in her hands. She's grinning.

"Daniel and Holder, sittin' in a tree," she says in a singsong voice.

I walk toward her and improvise the next line of the song. "But then Daniel climbs down," I finish the rest of the sentence in a hurry, "and goes to Six's window and climbs inside her bedroom and throws her on the bed and kisses her until he can't take any more and has to go home and stroke his ego."

She's laughing and backing into her bedroom to make room for me to climb inside.

Once I'm inside, I look around and observe her room. I finally understand what she meant when she said my bedroom was more than just a room. This is like a secret glimpse into who Six really is. I feel like I could study this room and everything in it and find out everything I ever need to know about her.

Unfortunately, she's standing at the foot of her bed and she looks a little bit nervous and way more beautiful than I deserve, and I can't take my eyes off of her long enough to even study her bedroom.

I can't help but smile at her. I can already tell this is about to be the best anniversary I've ever had. The lights are off, so the mood is already perfect for making out. It's quiet, though. So quiet I can hear her breaths increase with each deliberately slow step I take toward her.

Shit. Maybe those are *my* breaths. I can't tell, because every inch closer I get requires an extra intake of air.

When I reach her, she's looking up at me with an odd mixture of peaceful anticipation. I want to push her onto the bed right now and climb on top of her and kiss the hell out of her.

I could do that, but why do the one thing she's expecting me to do?

I lean in slowly. Very slowly . . . until my mouth is so close to her neck she more than likely can't even tell if I'm touching her skin or not. "I have three questions I need to ask you before we do this," I say quietly, but very seriously. I pull back just far enough to see her gulp softly.

"Before we do what?" she asks hesitantly.

I lift a hand to the back of her head, then pull back from her neck and position my lips close to hers. "Before we do what we both want to do. Before I lean in one more inch. And before you part your lips for me just enough for me to steal a taste. Before I put my hands on your hips and back you up until you have nowhere to go but onto your bed."

I can feel her breath teasing my lips and it's so tempting I have to force myself to lean in to her ear again so I'm not so close to her mouth. "Before I slowly lower myself on top of you and our hands become curious and brave. Before my fingers slip under the hem of your shirt. Before my hand begins to explore its way up your stomach, and I discover I've never touched skin as soft as yours."

She gasps, then exhales a shaky breath and it's almost as sexy as the fist bump.

It may even be sexier.

"Before I finally get to touch your boob on *purpose*."

She laughs at that one, but her laugh is cut short when I press my thumb to the center of her lips.

"Before your breaths pick up pace and our bodies are aching because everything we're feeling is just making us want more and more and more of each other. Until I'm afraid I'll beg you not to ask me to slow down. So instead, I regrettably tear my mouth from yours and force myself away from your bed and you lift up unto your elbows and look at me, disappointed, because you kind of wished I would have kept going, but at the same time you're relieved I didn't, because you know you would have given in. So instead of giving in, we just stare. We watch each other silently as my heart rate begins to slow down and your breaths are easier to catch and the insatiable need is still there, but our minds are clearer now that I'm not pressed against you anymore. I turn around and walk to your window and leave without even saying good-bye, because we both know if either of us speaks . . . it'll be the collective demise of our willpower and we'll cave. We'll cave so hard."

I move my hand to her cheek. She whimpers and looks like she's about to collapse onto the bed, so I wrap my other arm around her lower back and pull her against me.

"So yeah . . . three questions first."

I let go of her and immediately turn around two seconds before I hear her fall onto her bed. I walk straight to the desk chair and take a seat, for two reasons. One, I want her to think I mean business and that everything I just said to her didn't affect me like it did her. And two, because I want her more than I've ever wanted anything and my knees were about to give out on me if I didn't sit down.

"Question number one," I say, watching her from across her room. She's lying on her back with her eyes closed and I hate that I'm not watching her up close right now. "When's your birthday?"

"October . . ." She clears her throat, obviously still recovering. "Thirty-first. Halloween."

How could the date of a birthday make me fall even harder for her? I have no idea, but it somehow does.

"Question number two. What's your favorite food?"

"Homemade mashed potatoes."

Never would have guessed that one. Glad I asked.

"Question number three," I say. "It's a big one. Are you ready?"

She nods, but keeps her eyes closed.

"What's the one thing in this room that tells the biggest secret about you?"

As soon as the question leaves my mouth, she's completely still. Her exaggerated breaths come to a halt. She remains motionless for almost a whole minute before she slowly pushes herself up until she's seated on the edge of the bed, facing me. "It has to be something inside this room?"

I nod slowly.

She lifts her hand and touches a finger to her heart, pointing at it. "This," she whispers. "My biggest secret is right in here."

Her eyes are moist and sad and somehow with that answer, the air instantly changes between us. In a dangerous way. A terrifying way. Because it feels like her air just became *my* air and I suddenly want to take in fewer breaths in order to ensure she never runs out.

I stand up and walk to the bed. Her eyes follow me closely until I'm directly in front of her. "Stand up."

She stands slowly.

I weave both hands through the locks of her hair until I'm holding the back of her head. I stare at her until my heart can't take anymore, then I press my lips to hers. I've lost count of how many times I've kissed her over the past day. Every time I kiss her, the feeling I get is like nothing I've ever experienced. The closest I've ever come to feeling this way is the day I was pretending to be in love with the girl in the closet. But even that day, the day I thought would surpass every day after it, doesn't come close to this.

Her mouth is warm and inviting and everything it always is when I kiss her, but it's also so much more. The fact that I have this reaction to her after one day scares the living shit out of me.

One day.

I've been doing this with her for one day and I have no idea what's happening. I don't know if it's a full moon or if I have a tumor wrapped around my heart or if she really is a witch. Whatever it is still doesn't explain how this kind of thing can exist between two people this ridiculously fast . . . and actually last.

I feel like deep down my heart knows she's too good to be true. My mind and my whole body know she's too good to be true, so I kiss her harder, hoping to convince myself that this is real. It's not some fairy tale. It's not an hour of make-believe.

This is reality, but even in our imperfect reality, people don't fall for each other like this. They don't develop feelings like this for someone they barely know.

The only thing my entire thought process is proving to me right now is how much I need to grab her tight and hang on, because wherever she goes, I want to go, too. And right now, she's going backward, down onto the bed. I'm easing myself on top of her in the same way I just told her this would happen. And we're kissing, just like I said we would, only this time it may just be a little more frantic and needy and holy *shit*.

Her skin.

It really is the softest skin I've ever touched.

I move my hand from her waist and inch my fingers underneath the hem of her shirt, then slowly begin to work my way to her stomach.

She pushes my hand away.

"Daniel."

She immediately lifts up and I immediately lift off her. She's breathing so heavily I catch myself holding my own breath, scared I'm hogging too much of her air.

She looks both regretful and embarrassed that she suddenly asked me to stop. I lift my hand and stroke her cheek reassuringly.

My eyes scroll over her features, taking in her nervous demeanor. She's afraid of what might happen between us. I can see on her face and in the way she's looking at me that she's just as scared as I am. Whatever this is between us, neither one of us was searching for it. Neither one of us knew it even existed. Neither one of us is even remotely prepared for it, but I know we both want it. She wants this to work with me as much as I want it to work with her and seeing the look in her eyes right now makes me believe that it will. I've never believed in anything like I believe in the possibility of the two of us.

I can tell by the way she's looking at me that if I tried to kiss her again, she'd let me. It's almost as if she's torn between the girl she used to be and the girl she is now and she's afraid if I try to kiss her again, she'll cave.

And I'm afraid if I don't get up and walk away, I'll let her.

We don't even have to speak. She doesn't even have to ask me to leave, because I know that's what I need to do. I nod, silently answering the question I don't want her to have to ask. I begin to ease off her bed and a silent *thank you* flashes in her eyes. I stand up, back away from her and climb out her window without a word. I walk a few feet until I reach the edge of her house, then I lean against it and slide down to the ground.

I lean my head back and close my eyes, attempting to figure out where I went right in my life to deserve her.

"What the hell are you doing?" Holder asks. I look up and he's halfway out Sky's window. Once he makes it all the way out, he turns and pulls her window shut.

"Recovering," I say. "I just needed a minute."

He walks toward me and takes a seat on the ground across from me, then leans against Sky's house. He pulls his legs up and rests his elbows on his knees.

"You're already leaving?" I ask him. "It's not even nine o'clock yet."

He reaches down to the ground and rips up a few blades of grass, then spins them between his fingers. "Got kicked out for the night. Karen walked in and my hand was up Sky's shirt. She didn't like that too much."

I laugh.

"So," he says, glancing back up at me. "You and Six, huh?"

Despite my effort not to smile, I do it anyway. I smile pathetically and nod. "I don't know what it is about her, Holder. I . . . she just . . . yeah."

"I know what you mean," he says quietly, looking back down at the grass between his fingers.

Neither one of us says anything else for several moments until he drops the blades of grass and wipes his hands on his jeans, preparing to stand up. "Well . . . I'm glad we had this talk, Daniel, but the fact that we already professed our mutual love for each other tonight is leaving me a little overwhelmed. I'll see you tomorrow." He stands up and begins walking toward his car.

"I love you, Holder!" I yell after him. "Best friends forever!"

He keeps walking forward, but lifts his hand in the air and flips me off.

It's almost as cool as a fist bump.

Chapter Five

"You're wrong," she says.

We're standing in my kitchen. Her back is pressed against the counter and I'm standing in front of her with my arms on either side of her. I catch her lips with mine and shut her up. It doesn't last long because she pushes my face away.

"I'm serious," she whispers. "I don't think they like me."

I bring a hand up and wrap it around the nape of her neck and look her directly in the eyes. "They like you. I promise."

"No we don't," my dad says as he makes his way into the kitchen. "We can't stand her. In fact, we hope you never bring her back." He refills his cup with ice, then walks back to the living room.

Six's eyes follow him as he exits the room, then she looks back up at me, wide-eyed.

"See?" I say with a smile. "They love you."

She points toward the living room. "But he just . . ."

My father's voice cuts her off when he walks back into the kitchen. "Kidding, Six," he says, laughing. "Inside joke. We actually like you a lot. I tried to give Danny-boy Grandma Wesley's ring earlier, but he says it's still too soon to make you a Wesley."

Six laughs at the same time she breathes a sigh of relief. "Yeah, maybe so. It's only been a month. I think we should wait at least two more weeks before we talk proposals."

My dad walks farther into the kitchen and leans against the counter across from us. I feel a little awkward standing so close to Six now, so I move next to her and lean against the bar.

"Did you come back in here so you could think of things to say that would embarrass me?" I ask. I know that's why he's standing here. I can see the glimmer in his eyes.

He takes a drink of his tea. He scrunches his nose up. "Nah," he says. "I would never do that, Danny-boy. I'm not the type of dad who would tell his son's girlfriend how he talks about her incessantly. I would also never tell my son's girlfriend that I'm proud of her for not having sex with him yet."

Holy shit. I groan and slap myself in the forehead. I should have known better than to bring her here.

"You talk to him about the fact that we haven't had sex?" Six says, completely embarrassed.

My father shakes his head. "No, he doesn't have to. I know because every night he comes home he goes straight to his bedroom and takes a thirty-minute shower. I was eighteen once."

Six covers her face with her hands. "Oh, my God." She peeks through her hands at my dad. "I guess I know who Daniel gets his personality from."

My father nods. "Tell me about it. His mother is terribly inappropriate."

Right on cue, my mother and Chunk walk through the front door with dinner. I glare at my father, then walk toward my mother and grab the pizza boxes out of her hands. She sets her purse down, walks over to Six, and gives her a quick hug.

"I'm sorry I didn't cook for you. Busy day today," she says.

"It's fine," Six replies. "Nothing like inappropriate conversation over pizza."

I watch as my mother spins around and eyes my father. "Dennis? What have you been up to?"

He shrugs. "Just telling Danny-boy how I would never embarrass him in front of Six."

My mother laughs. "Well, as long as you aren't embarrassing him, then. I'd hate for Six to find out about his lengthy showers every night."

I slap the table. "Mom! Jesus Christ!"

My dad winks at her. "Already covered that one."

Six walks to the table, shaking her head. "Your parents actually make you seem like a gentleman." She takes a seat at the table and I sit in the chair next to her.

"I'm so sorry," I whisper to her. She looks at me and smiles.

"Are you kidding me? I *love* this."

"Why would long showers embarrass you?" Chunk says to me, taking a seat across from Six. "I would think wanting to be clean is a good thing." She picks up a slice of pizza and begins to take a bite, but then her eyes squeeze shut and she drops the pizza onto her plate. By the look on her face, the meaning behind the long showers has just hit her. "Oh, gross. *Gross!*" she says, shaking her head.

Six begins to laugh and I rest my forehead against my hand, convinced this is more than likely the most uncomfortable, embarrassing five minutes of my life. "I hate all of you. Every last one of you." I quickly look at Six. "Except you, babe. I don't hate you."

She smiles and wipes her mouth with a napkin. "I know exactly what you mean. I hate everybody, too."

As soon as the words fall from her mouth, she looks away like she didn't just punch me in the gut, rip out my intestines, and stomp them into the ground.

I hate everybody too, Cinderella.

The words I said that day in the closet are screaming loudly inside my head.

There's no way.

There's no way I wouldn't have noticed she was Cinderella.

I bring my hands to my face and close my eyes, trying hard to remember something about that day. Her voice, her kiss, her smell. The way we seemed to connect almost instantly.

Her *laugh*.

"Are you okay?" Six asks quietly. No one else can tell something major is going on with me right now, but she notices. She notices because we're in sync. She notices because we have this unspoken connection. We've had it since the second I laid eyes on her in Sky's bedroom.

We've had it since the second she fell on top of me in the maintenance closet.

"No," I say, bringing my hands down. "I'm not okay." I grip the edge of the table, then slowly turn to face her.

Soft hair.

Amazing mouth.

Phenomenal kisser.

My mouth is dry, so I reach to my cup and down a huge gulp of water. I slam my cup back down on the table, then turn and face her. I'm trying not to smile, but this whole thing is slightly overwhelming. Realizing that the girl from my past that I wished I could know is the same girl from my present that I'm thankful to have is practically one of the best moments of my life. I want to tell Six, I want to tell Chunk, I want to tell my parents. I want to scream it from the rooftops and print it in all the papers.

Cinderella is Six! Six is Cinderella!

"Daniel. You're scaring me," she says, watching as my face grows paler and my heart pounds faster.

I look at her. *Really* look at her this time.

"You want to know why I haven't given you a nickname yet?"

She looks confused that this is what I decide to say in the middle of my silent freak-out. She nods cautiously. I place one hand on the back of her chair and one hand on the table in front of her, then lean in toward her.

"Because I already gave you one, Cinderella."

I pull back slightly and watch her face closely, waiting on the re-alization she's about to have. The flashback. The clarity. She's about to wonder how the hell she failed to realize it, too.

Her eyes slowly move up my face until they meet mine. "No," she says, shaking her head.

I nod slowly. "Yes."

She's still shaking her head. "No," she says again with more cer-tainty. "Daniel there's no way it could . . ."

I don't let her finish. I grab her face and kiss her harder than I've ever kissed her. I don't give a shit that we're seated at a dinner table. I don't care that Chunk is groaning. I don't care that my mom is clearing her throat. I keep kissing her until she begins to back away from me.

She's pushing on my chest, so I pull away from her just in time to see the regret wash over her entire face. I focus on her eyes long enough to see them squeeze shut as she stands to leave the kitchen. I watch her rush away long enough to see her stifle a sob by slapping her hand over her mouth. I remain in my seat until the front door slams shut and I realize she's gone.

I'm immediately out of my seat. I rush out the front door and run straight to her car, which is now backing out of my driveway. I slam my fist against her hood as I rush to catch up to her window. She's not looking at me. She's wiping tears away, trying her hardest not to look out the window I'm banging on.

"Six!" I yell, repeatedly banging on her window with my fist. I see her hand reach down to put the car in drive. I don't even think. I sprint to the front of the car and slap my hands down on the hood, standing directly in front of it so she can't take off. I'm watching her do everything she can to avoid looking at me.

"Roll down your window," I yell.

She doesn't move. She continues to cry as she focuses on everything other than what's right in front of her.

Me.

I slap the hood of the car again until she finally brings her eyes up to meet mine. Seeing her heartache confuses the hell out of me. I couldn't have been happier finding out she was Cinderella, yet she seems embarrassed as hell that I realized it.

"Please," I say, wincing from the ache that just reached my chest. I hate seeing her upset and I really hate that this is why she's upset.

She puts the car in park, then reaches a hand to her door and lowers the driver's side window. I'm not so sure she still won't drive away if I move out from in front of her car. I carefully and very slowly begin to make my way toward her window, the whole time keeping an eye on her hand to ensure she doesn't put the car back into drive.

When I reach her window, I bend my knees and lower myself until I'm face to face with her. "Do I even need to ask?"

She looks up at the roof and leans her head against the headrest. "Daniel," she whispers through her tears. "You wouldn't understand."

She's right.

She's absolutely right.

"Are you embarrassed?" I ask her. "Because we had sex?"

She squeezes her eyes shut, giving away the fact that she thinks I'm judging her. I immediately reach a hand through her window and pull her gaze back to mine. "Don't you dare be embarrassed by that. Ever. Do you know how much that meant to me? Do you know how many times I've thought about you? I was there. I made that choice right along with you, so please don't think for a second that I would ever judge you for what happened between us."

She begins to cry even harder. I want her to get out of the car. I need to hold her because I can't see her this upset and not do whatever I can to take it away.

"Daniel, I'm sorry," she says through her sobs. "This was a mistake. This was a huge mistake." Her hand reaches down to the gearshift and I'm already reaching into the car, trying to stop her.

"No. No, Six," I plead. She puts the car in drive and reaches to the door, then places her finger on the window button.

I make one last attempt to lean in and kiss her before the window begins to rise on me. "Six, *please*," I say, shocked at the sadness and desperation in my own voice. She continues to raise the window until I'm completely out of it and it's all the way up. I press my palms to her window and slap the glass, but she drives away.

There's nothing left for me to do but watch the back of the car as it disappears down the street.

What the hell was that?

I pull my hands through my hair and look up at the sky, confused as to what just happened.

That wasn't her.

I hate that she had the complete opposite reaction from me when she found out who I was.

I hate that she's embarrassed about that day, like she just wants to forget it. Like she wants to forget *me*.

I hate it because I've done everything I possibly can to commit that day to my memory, like no one or nothing else I've ever experienced.

She can't do this. She can't just push me away like this without an explanation.

Chapter Six

I couldn't give my parents an explanation when I went back inside to grab my keys. They were apologetic, thinking they did something wrong. They felt bad about their jokes, but I didn't even have it in me to reassure them that they weren't the problem. I couldn't reassure them, because I don't even know what the problem is.

I'll be damned if I don't find out tonight, though. Right now.

I put my car in park and turn off the engine, relieved to see her car parked in her driveway. I get out of my car and shut my door, then head to her front door. Before I make it to her front porch, I detour to the side of the house. I know with the shape she left my house in a few minutes ago, there's no way she would have walked through her front door. She would have taken the window.

I reach her bedroom and the window is shut, as well as the curtains. The room is dark, but I know she's inside. Knocking won't do me any good, so I don't even bother. I push the window up, then slide the curtains to the side.

"Six," I say firmly. "I'm respecting your window rule, but it's really hard right now. We need to talk."

Nothing. She says nothing. I know she's in her room, though. I can hear her crying, but barely.

"I'm going to the park. I want you to meet me there, okay?"

Several silent moments pass before she responds.

"Daniel, go home. Please." Her voice is soft and weak, but the message behind that sad, angelic voice is like a stab to my heart. I back away from the window, then kick the side of the house out of frustration. Or anger. Or sadness or . . . *shit*. All of it.

I lean back into her window and grip the frame. "Meet me at the goddamned park, Six!" I say loudly. My voice is angry. *I'm* angry. She's pissing me the hell off. "We don't do this kind of thing. You don't play these games. You owe me a fucking explanation."

I push away from her window and turn to walk back to my car. I make it five feet before my palms are running down my face and I'm wishing I could punch the actual air in front of me. I stop walking and pause for several moments while I search for patience. It's in here somewhere.

I walk back to her window and hate that she's crying much louder now, even though she's trying to stifle the sounds with her pillow.

"Listen, babe," I say quietly. "I'm sorry I said goddamned. And fucking. I shouldn't cuss when I'm upset, but . . ." I inhale a deep breath. "But *dammit*, Six. *Please. Please* just meet me at the park. If you aren't there in half an hour, I'm done. I had enough of this bullshit with Val and I'm not putting myself through it again."

I turn to leave and make it all the way to my car this time before pausing and kicking at the ground. I walk back to her window again. "I didn't mean it just now when I said I'd be done if you didn't show up. If you don't show up to the park, I'll still want to be with you. I'll just be sad that you didn't show up. Because we show up, Six. It's what we do. It's me and you, babe."

I wait for a reply for a lot longer than I even need to. She never responds, so I go back to my car and climb inside, then head to the park and hope she shows up.

•   •   •

Twenty-seven minutes pass before her car finally pulls into a parking spot.

I'm not surprised she showed up. I knew she would. Her reaction was uncharacteristic of her and I know she just needed time to let everything soak in.

I watch her as she slowly makes her way toward me, never once looking up at me. She keeps her eyes trained to the ground the whole time until she passes me. She sinks into the swing next to me and grabs the chains, then leans her head against her arm. I wait for her to speak first, knowing she more than likely won't.

She doesn't.

I run my hands up the chain rope until they're even with my head, then I lean into my arm and mirror her position. We're both staring quietly into the dark night in front of us.

"After you left that day," I say. "I wasn't sure of what you wanted me to do. I wondered if you thought about me, too, and if you had changed your mind. If maybe you wanted me to try and find you."

I tilt my head and look at her. Her blonde hair is tucked behind her ears and her eyes are closed. Even with her eyes closed I can see the pain in her features.

"For days I wondered if that's what you wanted me to do. I waited and waited for you to come back, but you never did. I know we both said we would be better off not knowing who the other was, but honestly, you were all I could think about. I wanted you to come back so fucking bad that I spent every single fifth period in that damn closet for the rest of the semester. The last day of school was the absolute worst. When the bell rang and I had to walk out of that closet for the last time, it absolutely sucked. So much. I felt like an idiot for being so consumed by the thought of you. When I met Val, I forced myself to go forward with her because it helped to not think about that damn closet so much."

I twist the swing until I'm facing her. "I like you, Six. A lot. And I know this sounds all kinds of jacked up and crazy, but pretending to make love to you that day was the closest I've ever been to actually loving someone until now."

I turn my swing to face forward again, then I stand up. I walk to her and kneel down on both knees in front of her, then wrap my arms around her waist. I look up at her and see the pain flash across her face when I touch her. "Six. Don't let what happened between us become a negative thing. *Please.* Because that day was one of the best days of my life. Actually, it was *the* best day of my life."

She lifts her head away from her arm and opens her eyes, then looks directly at me. Tears are streaming down her face. It breaks my damn heart.

"Daniel," she whispers through her tears. She squeezes her eyes shut and turns her head like she can't even look at me. "I got pregnant."

Chapter Seven

Sometimes when I'm almost asleep, I'll hear something that pulls me right back into a state of high alert. I'll listen closely, wondering if I actually heard a sound or if it's just my imagination playing tricks on me. I'll hold my breath and be really still, and I'll just listen quietly.

I'm quiet.

I'm still.

I'm holding my breath.

I'm listening.

I'm concentrating really hard while my head rests on her thighs. I don't know when I lowered it here, but my hands are still gripping her waist. I'm trying to figure out if those words are going to hit me and completely knock my heart around like a punching bag all over again, or if it was just my imagination.

God, I hope it was my imagination.

A tear hits my cheek that just fell straight from her eyes.

"I didn't find out until I was already in Italy," she says, her voice coated and laced with sorrow and shame. "I'm so sorry."

In my head, I'm counting backward. Counting the days and the weeks and the months and trying to make sense of what she's saying, because she's obviously not pregnant now. My mind is still churning, crunching numbers, erasing errors, crunching more numbers.

She was in Italy for almost seven months.

Seven months there, three months before she left and one month since she returned.

That's almost a year.

My mind hurts. Everything hurts.

"I didn't know what to do," she says. "I couldn't raise him by myself. I was already eighteen when I found out, so . . ."

I immediately lift up and look at her face. *"Him?"* I ask, shaking my head. "How do you know . . ." I close my eyes and blow out a steady breath, then release my grip on her waist. I stand up and turn around, then pace back and forth, absorbing everything that's happening.

"Six," I say, shaking my head. "I don't . . . are you saying . . ." I pause, then turn and face her. "Are you telling me you had a fucking *baby*? That *we* had a baby?"

She's crying again. Sobbing, even. Hell, I don't know if she ever even stopped. She nods like it's painful to do.

"I didn't know what to do, Daniel. I was so scared."

She stands up and walks toward me, then places her hands delicately on my cheeks. "I didn't know who you were, so I didn't know how to tell you. If I knew your name or what you looked like I never would have made that decision without you."

I bring my hands up to hers, and I pull them away from my face. "Don't," I say as I feel the resentment building within me. I'm trying so hard to hold it back. To understand. To let it all soak in.

I just can't.

"How could you not tell me? It's not like you found a puppy, Six. This is . . ." I shake my head, still not getting it. "You had a *baby*. And you didn't even bother telling me!"

She grasps my shirt in her fists, shaking her head, wanting me to see her side of things. "Daniel, that's what I'm trying to tell you! What was I supposed to do? Did you expect me to plaster flyers all over the school asking for information on who knocked me up in the maintenance closet?"

I look her directly in the eyes. "Yes," I say in a low voice.

She takes a step back, so I take a step forward. "*Yes*, Six! That's *exactly* what I would have expected you to do. You should have plastered it all over the hallways, aired it on the radio, taken an ad out in the motherfucking newspaper! You get pregnant with my kid and you worry about your *reputation*? Are you *kidding* me?"

My hand covers my cheek a second after she slaps me.

The pain in her eyes can't even come close to matching the pain in my heart, so I don't feel bad for saying what I said. Even when she begins to cry harder than I knew people were capable of crying.

She rushes back to her car.

I let her go.

I walk back to the swing and I sit.

Fucking life.

Motherfucking life.

Daniel: Where are you?

Holder: Just left Sky's house. Almost home. What's up?

Daniel: I'll be there in five.

Holder: Everything okay?

Daniel: Nope.

Five minutes later Holder is standing on his curb waiting for me. I pull onto the side of the street and he opens the passenger door, then climbs inside. I put my car in park and prop my foot on the dash, then look out my window.

I'm surprised at how pissed I am. I'm even surprised at how sad I am. I don't know how to separate everything I'm feeling in order to get a grip on the core of what's upsetting me the most. Right now I can't tell if it's the fact that I didn't have a say in whatever decision she made or if it's because she was even put into that situation to have to make that kind of decision to begin with.

I'm pissed I wasn't there to help her. I'm pissed I was careless enough to make a girl go through something like that.

I'm sad because . . . *hell*. I'm sad that I'm so mad at her. I'm sad I have to know something this overwhelming and there isn't a damn thing I can do about it now, even if I wanted to. I'm sad because I'm sitting here in a parked car and I'm about to have a breakdown in front of my best friend and I really don't want to do that but it's too late.

I punch the steering wheel the second I begin to cry. I punch it several times, over and over, until the car begins to close in on me and I need to get the hell out of it. I open the door and climb out, then turn around and kick my tire. I kick it over and over until my foot starts to go numb, then I collapse against the hood onto my elbows. I press my forehead against the cold metal of the car and focus on burying this anger.

It's not her fault.

It's not her fault.

It's not her fault.

When I'm finally calm enough to return to the car, Holder is sitting quietly in the passenger seat, watching me closely.

"You want to talk about it?" he asks.

I shake my head. "Nope."

He nods. He's probably relieved I don't want to talk about it.

"What do you want to do?" he asks.

I wrap my fingers around the steering wheel, then crank the car. "I don't care what we do."

"Me neither."

I put the car in drive.

"We could go to Breckin's house and let you get your aggression out on a video game," he suggests.

I nod, then begin to drive toward Breckin's house. "You better not fucking tell him I cried."

Chapter Eight

"You look like hell," Holder says, leaning against the locker next to mine. "Did you even sleep last night?"

I shake my head. Of course I didn't. How the hell could I have slept? I knew she wasn't sleeping, so there's no way in hell I could have.

"You gonna tell me what happened?" he asks. I shut my locker, but keep my hand on it as I look down at the floor and slowly inhale.

"No. I know I usually tell you everything, but not this, Holder."

He taps the locker next to him a couple of times with his fist, then he pushes off of it. "Six isn't telling Sky anything, either. Not sure what happened, but . . ." He looks at me until I make eye contact with him. "I like you with her. Get it worked out, Daniel."

He walks away and I close my locker. I wait next to it for a few minutes more than necessary because my next class is down the hall-way where Six's locker is. I haven't seen her since she left the park last night and I'm not sure I really want to see her. I'm not sure about anything. I have so many questions, but just thinking about having to ask her any of them makes my chest hurt so bad I can't fucking breathe.

After the final bell rings, I decide to walk to my next class. I debated staying home from school altogether, but I figured it would be worse just sitting in my room thinking about it all day. I'd rather be preoccupied for as long as I can today because I know as soon as school is out I need to confront her.

Or maybe I'm supposed to confront her right now, because as soon as I round the corner, my eyes land on her.

I come to a quiet stop and watch her. She's the only one in the hallway. She's standing still, facing her locker. I want to walk away before she sees me, but I can't stop watching her. Her whole demeanor is heartbroken and I want so bad to rush over to her and wrap my arms around her but . . . I can't. I want to scream at her and hug her and kiss her and blame her for every single jumbled-up emotion I've spent the last day trying to process.

I sigh heavily and she turns to look at me. I'm far enough away that I can't hear her crying, but close enough I can see the tears. Neither one of us moves. We just stare. Several moments pass and I can see she's hoping I say something to her.

I clear my throat and begin walking toward her. The closer I get, the louder her soft cry becomes. I get about five feet away, then I pause. The closer I get to her, the harder it is to breathe.

"Is he . . ." I close my eyes and pass a calming breath, then open them again and try my hardest to finish my sentence with dry eyes. "When you talked about the boy who broke your heart in Italy . . . you were referring to him, weren't you? The baby?"

I can barely see the nod of her head when she confirms my thoughts. I squeeze my eyes shut and tilt my head back.

I didn't know hearts could literally ache like this. It hurts so much I want to reach inside and rip it out of my chest so I'll never feel this again.

I can't do this. Not right here. We can't stand in the hallway of a high school and have this discussion.

I turn around before I open my eyes so I don't have to see the look on her face again. I walk straight to my classroom and open the door, then walk inside without looking back at her.

Chapter Nine

I don't know why I'm still here. I don't want to be here and I'm pretty sure I'll leave in half an hour. I just can't leave before then because I'm scared of what she might think if I don't show up to lunch. I could text her and tell her I'll talk to her later, but I'm not even sure I feel like sending her a text yet. There's still so much I have to process, I'd rather just ignore it all until I find the strength to sort through everything.

I walk through the cafeteria doors and head straight to our table. There's no way I can eat lunch so I don't even bother getting food. Breckin is sitting in my usual spot next to Six, but that's probably a good thing. Not so sure I could sit by her right now, anyway.

Her eyes are focused on the textbook in front of her. She's not crying anymore. I take a seat across from her and I know she knows I just sat down, but her eyes never move. Sky and Holder are deep in conversation with Breckin, so I watch them, trying to find a spot to jump in.

I can't though, because I'm completely unable to pay attention. I keep stealing glances at her to make sure she isn't crying or to see if she's looking at me. She never does either of those things.

"You're not eating?" Breckin says, catching my attention.

I shake my head. "Not hungry."

"You need to eat something," Holder says. "And a nap might do you some good, too. Maybe you should go home."

I nod, but don't say anything.

"If you do go home, you should take Six with you," Sky says. "You both look like you could use a nap."

I don't even respond to that with a nod. My eyes fall back to Six just in time to see a tear land on a page in front of her. She quickly swipes it away with her hand and flips the page over.

Fuck if that just didn't make me feel like complete shit.

I continue to watch her and tears continue to fall onto the pages, one by one. Her hand is always quick to wipe them away before anyone notices and she always flips to a new page before she can even possibly have read the last one.

"Get up, Breckin," I say. He looks at me blankly, but doesn't make an effort to move. "I want your seat. Get up."

He finally realizes what I'm saying, so he quickly stands up. I stand and walk around the table. I sit down beside her and when I do, she brings her arms onto the table. She folds them and buries her head into the crease in her elbow. I watch as her shoulders begin to shake and dammit if I can allow her to keep feeling this way. I wrap an arm around her and lower my forehead to the side of her head and I close my eyes. I don't say anything. I don't do anything. I just hold her while she cries into her arms.

"Daniel," I hear her say through her muffled tears. She lifts her head and looks up at me. "Daniel, I'm so sorry. I'm so, so sorry." Her tears become sobs and her sobs become too much. It's too fucking much.

I pull her to my chest. "Shh," I say into her hair. "Don't. Don't apologize."

Her body becomes limp against mine and everyone in the cafeteria is beginning to stare at us. I want to hold her and tell her how sorry I am for allowing her to walk away last night, but she needs privacy. I wrap my arm tighter around her, then scoop her legs up into my other arm. I pull her against me, then stand up and carry her out into the hallway. I keep walking until I round the corner and find our room. She's still crying against my chest, wrapped tightly around me. I open the door to the maintenance closet, then I close it behind us. I back up to the door and slide down until I meet the floor, still holding her in my arms.

"Six," I say, lowering my mouth to her ear. "I want you to try to stop crying, because I have so much I want to say to you."

I feel her nod against my chest and I remain quiet, waiting on her to calm down. Several minutes pass before she's finally quiet enough for me to continue.

"First of all, I am so sorry for letting you walk away last night, but I don't want you to think for one second it was because I was judging your choices. Okay? I'm not about to put myself in your shoes and tell you that you made a bad choice, because I wasn't there and I have no clue how hard that must have been for you."

I adjust her and straighten out my legs so she's forced to sit up and look at me. I pull one of her legs to the other side of me until she's facing me. "I'm just sad, okay? That's all this is. I'm allowed to be sad about this and I need you to let me be sad because this is a whole hell of a lot to process in a day."

She pulls her lips into a thin line and she nods while I wipe away her tears with both my thumbs. "I have so many questions, Six. And I know you'll answer them when you're ready, but I can wait. If you need me to give you time I can."

She shakes her head. "Daniel. He's your son. I'll answer any question you ask me. I just don't know if you want to hear the answers because . . ." She squeezes her eyes shut to hold back more tears. "Because I think I made the wrong choice and it's too late. It's too late to go back now."

She's crying hard again, so I wrap my arms around her and hug her.

"If I knew he was yours or that I would eventually find you I would have never done it, Daniel. I would have never given him up.

But I did and now you're here and it's too late because I don't know where he is and I'm sorry. God, I'm so sorry."

I shake my head, wishing she would stop. It's hurting me more to see her upset with herself than anything else about this whole situation.

"Listen to me, Six." I pull back and look her in the eyes, holding her face firmly between my hands. "You made a choice for *him*. Not for yourself. Not for me. You did what was best for him and I will never be able to thank you enough for that. And please don't think this changes how I feel about you. If anything, it just lets me know that I'm not crazy. For the past month I've been thinking my feelings for you couldn't be real because there are so many of them and they're so much. *Too* much sometimes. I constantly have to bite my tongue when I'm around you because all I've been wanting to do lately is tell you how much I love you. But it's only been a month since we met and the only other time I've said those words out loud to a girl was over a year ago. Right here on this floor. And you wouldn't believe how real I wanted that moment to be for us, Six. I know I didn't know you but my *God*, I wished I did. And now that I do know you . . . *really* know you . . . I know it's real. I love you. And knowing what we shared last year and now knowing what you had to go through and how it's made you exactly who you are right now . . . it just blows my mind. It blows my mind that I get to love you."

I feel her hands wiping tears from my cheeks when I lean in to kiss her. I pull her against me and she pulls me against her and I have no plans to ever let her go. I kiss her until her hands move up to my face and she pulls her lips from mine. Our foreheads meet and she's still crying, but her tears are different now. I feel like they're tears of relief rather than tears of worry.

"I'm so happy it's you," she says, keeping her hands locked on my face. "I'm so happy it was you."

I pull her against me and hold her. I hold her for so long that the bell rings and the hallway fills and empties and another bell rings and we're still sitting here together, holding on to each other when the silence in the hallway returns. I'm periodically pressing kisses into her hair, stroking her back, kissing her forehead.

"He looked like you," she says quietly. Her hand is lightly trailing up and down my arm and her cheek is pressed against my chest. "He had your brown eyes and he was kind of bald, but I could tell he was going to have brown hair. And he had your mouth. You have a great mouth."

I rub my hand up her back and kiss the top of her head. "He's got it made," I say. "Looks just like his daddy, hopefully acts like his mommy, and he'll have a nice Italian accent. Kid won't have any problems in life."

She laughs and hearing that sound immediately brings tears to my eyes again. I squeeze her tight against me, rest my cheek against the top of her head, and sigh.

"It's probably for the best that it all happened like it did," I say. "If we had decided to keep him I would have ruined him with some stupid nickname. I probably would have called him Salty Balls or some shit like that. I'm not cut out to be a dad yet, obviously."

She shakes her head. "You'd be a great dad. And one of these days, Salty Balls will be the perfect nickname for one of our kids. Just not yet."

Now I'm the one laughing. "What if we have all girls?"

She shrugs. "Even better."

I smile and keep her held close against me. After last night and being apart from her, knowing how much she was hurting, I know I'll never want to feel that way again. I never want *her* to feel that way again.

"You know what I just realized?" she says. "We've already had sex. I've been kind of bummed because if I had sex with you, it would have made you the seventh person I've ever had sex with and that's a lot. But you'll still be the sixth, because I was already counting you and I didn't even know it."

"I like six," I say. "That's a good number to be. It's actually my favorite number."

"Don't get too excited now that you know we've already had sex," she says. "I'm still making you wait."

"I'll wear you down soon enough," I tease.

I bring one of my hands up to her head and I hold it while I lean forward and kiss her softly on the lips. I stay close to her mouth and make a confession. "I haven't brought this up because we haven't been together that long and I didn't want to scare you off. But now that I know we have a kid together, it makes it less embarrassing."

"Oh, no. What is it?" she asks nervously.

"We graduate in less than a month. I know you and Sky and Holder were planning on going to the same college in Dallas after the summer. I had already applied to a college in Austin, but after I met you I might have applied to Dallas, too. You know . . . in case things worked out with us. I didn't like the thought of being five hours apart."

She tilts her head and looks up at me. "When did you apply?"

I shrug like it's not a big deal. "The night Sky had that dinner for you."

She sits up and looks at me. "That was twenty-four hours after we went out for the first time. You applied to my college after knowing me for one day?"

I nod. "Yeah, but technically I knew you for a whole year. If you look at it that way, it's way less creepy."

She smiles at my logic. "Well? Did you get accepted?"

I nod. "I might have already made living arrangements with Holder, too."

She grins and it's probably the most I've ever loved a smile. "Daniel? This is serious. This thing with us. It's pretty intense, huh?"

I nod. "Yeah. I think we might really be in love this time. No more pretending."

She nods. "Things are so serious now, I think it's time I introduced you to all my brothers."

I stop nodding and start shaking my head back and forth. "I may be exaggerating. I don't love you *that* much."

She laughs. "No, you love me. You love me so much, Daniel. You've loved me since the second I let you accidentally touch my boob."

"No, I think I've loved you since you forced me to stick my tongue in your mouth."

She shakes her head. "No, you've loved me since I let you kiss me in a crowded restaurant next to a dirty diaper."

"Nope. I've loved you since you walked through Sky's bedroom door with that spoon in your mouth."

"Actually, you've loved me since the first time you told me you loved me a year ago. Right here in this room."

I shake my head. "I've loved you since the moment you fell on top of me and said you hated everybody."

She stops smiling. "I've loved you since the moment you said you hated everybody, too."

"I used to hate everybody," I say. "Until I met you."

"I told you I was unhateable." She grins.

"And I told you unhateable isn't even a real word."

Her eyes focus on mine and she takes both my hands, then laces her fingers through them. We stare at each other like we've done so many times before, but this time I feel it in every single part of me. I feel *her* in every part of me and the feeling is new and heavy and intense. I realize in this moment that we just became so much more together than we could ever possibly be alone.

"I love you, Daniel Wesley," she whispers.

"I love you Seven Marie Six Cinderella Jacobs."

She laughs. "Thank you for not turning out to be an asshole."

"Thank you for never asking me to change." I lean forward and kiss the smile that just spread across her lips as I silently thank the universe for sending her back to me.

My fucking angel.

Epilogue

"What in the world is wrong with you, Daniel?" Chunk says, slapping her pen down on the table.

I pause the drumming of my fingers against the wooden tabletop. "Nothing." I didn't realize my nervousness was so obvious. Especially to a thirteen-year-old.

"Something's wrong with you," she says. She pushes her homework aside and folds her arms across the table, leaning forward. "Did you break up with Six?"

I shake my head. "No."

"She break up with you?"

"*Hell* no," I say defensively.

"Get in trouble at school?"

I shake my head and look down at the time on my phone. Ten more minutes and I'll leave. I just need ten more minutes.

"You get her pregnant?" Chunk asks.

My eyes dart up to hers and my pulse increases. I technically can't answer that with a no, because . . . well.

"Oh, my god," Chunk says. "You got her pregnant? Daniel! Mom and Dad are gonna *kill* you!"

She pushes away from the table just as my mother walks into the kitchen. Chunk's hands go up to her mouth in disbelief and she's shaking her head, still staring at me. She doesn't know my mother is behind her now. "Daniel, are you stupid? I'm only thirteen, but even *I* know what safe sex is. Christ, I can't believe you got her *pregnant*!"

I'm shaking my head, too flustered to tell her Six isn't pregnant.

My mother is frozen, staring at me with wide eyes. She covers her mouth with her hand at the same moment my father walks into the kitchen. Chunk hears him and spins around.

"What's wrong?" my father asks. "You all look like you've seen a ghost."

Before I have the chance to defend myself or dismiss the words that just came out of Chunk's mouth, my mother turns to face my father. She points at me.

"He got her pregnant," she whispers disbelievingly. "Your son got his girlfriend pregnant."

My father stares silently at my mother. I know I should be standing up right now—denying everything before they all get too worked up, but everything they're saying is technically true.

I *did* get Six pregnant.

However, that was over a year ago and none of them know about that, nor do they *need* to know about it. But Six sure as hell isn't pregnant right now. I know that for a fact. We've been dating for over three months, and I'm sure it'll be at least three more months before she allows me to break that bread.

I don't like that analogy. Doesn't even make sense.

Jump that fence?

Nah, that's not sexy enough.

Cross that finish line?

Nope. It'll be more like a starting *line.*

Tap that ass?

Meh. Too tacky.

Poke that potato?

"Daniel?" my father asks, pulling my gaze to his. He doesn't look happy, but he also doesn't look angry. Which is weird, since he's just been told he'll likely be a grandfather, and he's only forty-five. He's looking at me like he's confused. "How can Six be pregnant?" he asks, shaking his head. "Every time you're with her you still come home and take those embarrassingly long showers."

I swear to God. Why do these people continue to bring that up?

I look over at Chunk and shake my head. "Six isn't pregnant," I tell all of them. "Chunk just has an overactive imagination."

A collective sigh comes from the three of them. My mother slaps her hand to her heart and releases a quick "Oh dear good lord, Jesus Christ, holy shit, thank *god!*" She blows out a calming breath after her slew of blasphemy.

Chunk rolls her eyes when she realizes I'm telling the truth. She takes her seat across from me and pulls her homework back in front of her. "Well, if she's not pregnant then what in the heck are you so nervous about?"

Oh yeah. This little distraction almost helped me forget everything that's about to happen. As soon as the night's plans invade my mind again, I have to inhale slowly through my nose to remind my lungs they need air.

"What is it, Danny boy?" my father asks. "She break up with you?"

I drop my head into my hands, frustrated at how damn nosey they all are.

"No," I groan. "She didn't break up with me. I also didn't break up with her. She's not pregnant, we aren't having sex, and I didn't get in trouble at school!" I'm standing now, pacing back and forth. The three of them are watching me practically have a meltdown. I finally turn and face them with my hands planted firmly on my hips. "I'm just freaking out a little bit, okay? I'm supposed to be at her house right now, because she wants me to meet her brothers. *All* of them. Like *right now.*"

My father looks amused, and it kind of pisses me off.

"How many brothers does she have?" my mother asks. Her voice is soothing, like she's about to give me the pep talk I'm desperately in need of.

"Four. And they're all older than she is."

My mother's mouth presses into a thin line as she gently nods her head. "Oh, boy," she says in a whisper. "You're screwed, Daniel." She turns around and walks into the kitchen. I'm stuck in the same position, wondering where her words of advice went.

My father is nodding his head, still with that annoying smile plastered on his face. "I really don't like Six," he says. "I'm starting to hate her, actually. Three months now, and she's *still* holding firm to that trophy?"

"Stop, Dad," I say immediately. "You are *not* allowed to talk about my sex life. And you're especially not allowed to use shitty analogies to reference the fact that Six is making me wait."

He holds his palms up defensively. "Sorry." He laughs. "Besides, I forget that your sister isn't an adult sometimes." He pats Chunk on her shoulder. "Sorry, Chunk. I'll never mention in front of you again how your brother's girlfriend won't allow him to kill that mocking-bird." He pulls out a chair and sits at the table. Chunk and I groan at the same time.

"Dad," she says. "You just ruined my favorite book with that comparison. Thanks a lot."

He winks at her before turning to face me again. "You'll be fine, Danny boy. Just don't be yourself at all, and they'll have no choice but to love you."

I grab my jacket off the back of the chair and pull it on as I exit the kitchen. "You all still suck," I mumble as I walk out the front door.

•   •   •

I don't remember walking into her house. I don't remember anything I said as I was being introduced to any of them. I don't even remember how I made it to my seat, but here I am—being stared down across the kitchen table by four of the most intimidating men I've ever met. I was hoping we were going to make it through the meal with everyone stuffing his face and no one addressing me directly.

That didn't even last a whole bite.

One of them just asked what my plans are after graduation, but I'm not sure which one he is. He's the one who looks the most like Six because he's the only blond, but he's also the largest of the four. His hands make his fork look like a toothpick.

I look down at my hands and frown, because they make my fork look like a spatula. I set my fork down on the table before they notice how tiny they all make my hands look.

Six taps my leg under the table, reminding me to speak. I gently clear my throat. "I'm not sure."

My voice sounds like a damn child's, compared to the four of their voices. I've never even thought about my voice or how it might sound to an outsider until this moment. I've never really thought about how my hands might make a fork look until now, either. I've also never really thought about breaking up with Six before, but . . . *nah*. I don't care how scary they are or how much they hate me. There's no way in hell I'm breaking up with Six.

"Well, are you at least going to college?" Evan asks.

I know Evan's name. He's the one closest in age to Six. He's also the only one who smiled at me when he introduced himself, so I made sure to remember him. That way, if the other three decide to jump me, I can scream Evan's name for help, since he'd be the only one likely to defend me.

"I am going to college," I say with a nod. *Finally. A question I can answer.* "I'm attending the same one Six will be at."

Evan nods his head slowly, digesting that response with a bite of food.

"What if the two of you aren't dating after graduation?" the big one says.

"Aaron, shut up," Six says with a roll of her eyes. She squeezes my leg under the table. "Stop antagonizing him."

Aaron's eyes are still locked with mine. "Do you think I'm antagonizing you?" he asks coolly. "I just thought we were having polite conversation."

I swallow the lump in my throat and shake my head. "You're fine," I say. "I get it. I have two sisters. Granted, one of them is older than me but I still give the douchebags she brings home a hard time. And don't even get me started on Chunk. The first guy she brings home doesn't stand a chance. I already hate him, and the kid probably doesn't even know she exists yet."

The brother directly across from me smiles a little bit. It might be my imagination, but I know for a fact he's not frowning anymore.

"Chunk?" Aaron asks. "Six said you give nicknames to people. That's what you call your little sister?"

I nod.

"What do you call Six?" the brother across from me says. I'm pretty sure his name is Michael. I have a fifty-fifty chance of being right, considering the brother on the end could also be named Michael. It's either that or Zachary.

Six bumps my leg again, and I realize I haven't answered him. "Cinderella," I blurt out.

They're all staring at me now, waiting for an explanation for that one. I don't think I want to give them one. How do you tell four brothers that you call their little sister Cinderella because you had random hot sex with her in the maintenance closet of a school?

"Why do you call her that?" Aaron asks. He turns toward the brother at the end. "Zach, didn't you used to have a turtle named Cinderella?"

Zach. Zach is the quietest one.

He shakes his head. "Ariel," he says, correcting Aaron. "I had a thing for the little mermaid."

The one I can now assume is Michael, based on the process of elimination, says, "You didn't answer the question. Why do you call her Cinderella?"

Six laughs under her breath, and I know she finds this extremely amusing, even though I sort of wish I would choke to death on a turkey bone so I could be put out of my misery.

"I call her Cinderella because the first time I laid eyes on her, I thought she was so beautiful she couldn't be real. Girls like her were reserved for fairy tales and fantasies."

I'm proud of my own answer. Didn't know I could bullshit under pressure like this.

The quiet one straightens up in his seat. *Zach.* "So you're saying you fantasize about our little sister?"

What the . . .

"Jesus, Zach!" Six yells. "Stop it! All four of you, stop it! You're just interrogating him to amuse yourselves."

All four of them begin to laugh. Evan winks at me, and they all begin eating again.

I'm still not brave enough to pick up my fork in front of them.

"We're just messing with you," Zach says with a laugh. "We never get to do this, because you're the first guy Six has ever let us meet."

I turn and look at Six. I didn't know this little fact, and I think I kind of love it. "Am I, really?" I ask her. "You've never introduced anyone to your brothers before?"

Six smiles and gives her head a small shake. "Why would I?" she says. "No other guy has ever deserved to meet them."

I immediately pull her to me, and I give her a loud smack on the lips. "Dammit, I love you, girl," I say, finding the confidence to finally pick up my fork again. It looks like a fork now rather than a spatula.

I dig in to the food and take a huge bite.

All four of her brothers are quietly staring back at me.

All four are smiling.

• • •

I fall onto Sky's bed with a huge sigh, landing on my back next to Holder, who is propped up against the headboard.

"I see you survived the meeting of the brothers," he says, looking down at me.

"Barely," I say. "But I think I won them over in the end."

"How'd you manage that?" Sky asks. She's sitting on the other side of Holder, messing with her phone.

"I gave them all nicknames. They found me highly amusing."

Holder laughs. "Only you, Daniel."

"Where's Six?" Sky asks me.

"She didn't feel like coming over." I pull myself up to a standing position. "I just wanted to let Holder know I'm still alive. I'm gonna head back over there."

Before I walk back to her bedroom window, I see a frown form on Sky's face. I don't like it, because she never frowns. She's one of the happiest people I've ever met.

Come to think of it, I also didn't like the fact that Six didn't want to come over here tonight. It was weird, because she didn't feel like it last night, either.

It hits me that something is up between the two of them.

"What's wrong, Cheese Tits?"

Her eyes shoot up to mine and she forces a smile. "Nothing."

I take a step back toward the bed. "I call bullshit," I say. "When's the last time you spoke to my girl?"

She glances down at her phone again and shrugs. Holder sees what I've noticed, and he puts an arm around her.

"Hey," he says reassuringly. "What's wrong, babe?" He pulls her in close to him and kisses her on the side of the head, just as a tear falls from her eyes. She quickly pulls her hand up to wipe it away, but Holder notices. He sits up straighter and turns to face her at the same time I take a seat back down on the bed.

"Sky, what's wrong?" he says, urging her to look up at him.

She shrugs it off, shaking her head. "It's probably nothing," she says. "I'm sure she's just tired or something."

"Who's tired?" I ask her. "Six?"

She nods.

Her assumption confuses me, because Six isn't tired. She seemed fine tonight.

"It's just that she hasn't been over here in the three days we've been out for Christmas break," Sky says. "She also hasn't texted or called me back. I think she's mad at me, but I have no idea what I did."

I immediately stand up. "Well, we have to fix this," I say, somewhat panicked. "She can't be mad at you. Y'all aren't allowed to fight." I begin pacing the room. Holder is watching me with those narrowed, intimidating eyes of his.

"Daniel, calm down. They're girls. Girls argue sometimes."

I shake my head, refusing to accept it. I'm pacing again. "Not Sky and Six. They aren't like all the other girls, Holder. You know that. They don't fight. They *can't* fight. We're supposed to go to college together. They're supposed to be roommates." I turn and face him, coming to a pause. "We're a team, man. Me and Six and you and Sky. Me and you. Six and Sky. They can't break up. I won't let it happen." I'm already heading to the window. Sky is pleading with me not to make a big deal out of it, but it's too late for that. I'm climbing in Six's bedroom window and my heart is racing, and there's no way I can let them keep this up for another day.

Six is lying on her bed, staring up at the ceiling. She doesn't turn to look at me when I enter her room. "What's the matter?" I ask her.

"Nothing," she says immediately.

Bullshit.

I kneel down on the bed and move toward her until I'm on top of her, looking down at her face. "Bullshit."

She turns away from me, so I grab her chin and make her look at me again. "Why are you mad at Sky?"

She shakes her head, and I can see in her eyes that she isn't mad at Sky. "I'm not mad at her," she says, sounding offended. I want to feel relieved, but something is still bothering her.

She looks worried. Scared, even. I feel like an asshole for not recognizing it earlier, but she *was* more quiet than usual during dinner.

And last night. She was really quiet last night.

Shit. Maybe she's mad at *me.*

"I'm sorry," I tell her. She looks up at me, confused.

"For what?"

I shrug. "I don't know. For whatever I did. Sometimes I do or say really stupid shit, and I don't even realize I'm doing it until I hurt someone's feelings. So if that's what's wrong, I'm sorry." I lower my head and kiss her. "I'm really, really sorry."

She pushes against my chest, and I sit back on my knees. She pulls herself to a seated position in front of me. "You didn't do anything wrong, Daniel. You're perfect."

I love that answer, but hate that I still don't know what's upsetting her.

"It's just that . . ." Her voice grows quiet, and she looks down at her lap. "If I tell you something . . . you swear you'll never ever tell Holder?"

I immediately nod my head. As much as I'll always be there for Holder, there's no way in hell I'd ever break Six's trust. "I swear."

Her eyes meet mine, and she's silently telling me I better be serious, because whatever she's about to tell me is a big deal.

I don't like this look in her eyes. Luckily, she scoots off the bed and walks to her desk. She picks up her laptop and brings it back to the bed with her. "I want to show you something." She opens the laptop and pulls up a minimized screen before turning it to face me. "And please never bring this up again, Daniel."

I pull the laptop in front of me and begin reading.

Words like *missing child* and *reward* and dates and statements and pictures are all flooding my eyes. I'm shaking my head, because the words on the screen don't make any sense when they're referring to the picture of the little girl who looks just like Sky.

"What is this, Six?" I ask.

She pulls the laptop back out of my hands. "I'm not sure," she says. "I left my computer here while I was in Italy. I just noticed a few days ago that this was in my search history from several months ago. I don't know what to do, Daniel," she says, looking down at the screen. "It's her. This is Sky. I would ask her about it, but I think if she knew about it, she would have said something to me."

I'm still trying to process what I just saw on the computer and all the words coming out of Six's mouth.

"What if it was Karen who used my computer? Or Holder? Or someone else entirely? I don't know for sure that Sky was the one looking this up, and I'm scared if I say anything to her, I'll be bringing up something she doesn't even want to know."

I don't even hesitate. I grab the laptop and stand up. "Six? This isn't something you keep to yourself. If you don't tell her now, nothing will ever be the same between the two of you, because you'll feel too guilty to talk to her." I grab her hand. "Come on. Let's just rip off the Band-Aid."

Her eyes are wide and scared, but I don't care. She can't keep something like this bottled up. And if this little girl really is Sky, she has every right to know.

We stand up but before we head to the window, I pull Six in for a tight hug. I kiss her on top of the head and tell her it'll be fine. "It might not even have anything to do with her," I say. "It could just be a coincidence."

$$\bullet \quad \bullet \quad \bullet$$

We're standing at the foot of Sky's bed, watching her. Holder has the laptop and Sky's hand is covering her mouth. They're both staring wide-eyed at the screen.

They're both quiet.

"I'm sorry," Six says. "I don't know what it is or who was looking it up . . . but I didn't know how to tell you. I also didn't know how *not* to tell you."

Sky finally pulls her eyes away from the computer, but they don't fall on Six. They slide up to Holder's face. He looks at her calmly and expels a deep breath, then gently closes the laptop.

Their reactions are way too weird. I expected a little crying. A little bit of yelling, maybe. Perhaps a few flying objects I'd have to duck from.

Holder pushes the laptop back toward Six. "We don't need to see it," he says. "She already knows."

Six gasps, and I grab her hand. Sky stands up at the same time Holder does. She walks toward us and places her hands on Six's shoulders, looking at her calmly. "I would have told you, Six," she says. "But if this ever gets out . . . it's not me that would be affected. It's Karen. That's the only reason I haven't told you."

Six's eyes are wide and hurt, but I can tell she's also trying to be understanding. "So it was Karen?" Six whispers, backing away from Sky.

Sky nods her head. "Everything you read about my childhood was true," she says. She looks at Holder for permission to continue. He nods, but looks at me and shoots me that look. The look that tells me that whatever I'm about to hear will never leave this room.

"Karen did what she had to do because my father was a monster," Sky says. Tears fill her eyes and Holder steps up behind her and places his hands on her shoulders. He kisses the top of her head, pulling her back against his chest. "I found out everything after Holder told me. While you were in Italy."

I look over at Holder. "How did *you* know?"

He regards me silently for a few seconds. He looks as if he regrets not telling me, but I don't blame him. It's not my business. "I recognized her. Me and Les . . . we used to live next door to them before we moved here. We were all friends. I was there when it happened."

Six and I both begin to pace the room. It's too much to take in. I'm not sure I even want to know something like this about them. That's a lot of pressure . . . having this kind of knowledge in my head. I don't like that they know I know this now. I liked how things were yesterday. I liked how easy it was, before all this new information was planted in my head. Now I have to bury it and pretend it's not there, but it's so huge. It's too much for Sky and Holder to have to trust us with this kind of thing.

"I got Six pregnant!" I blurt out, feeling somewhat relieved that I'm giving them a secret, too. "Last year. She was the girl in the closet," I say to Holder. I told him about her once before, so I know he'll know what I'm referring to. "We had sex without even knowing what the other looked like. She got pregnant and found out when she was in Italy. She didn't know who I was and she was scared, so she gave our son up for adoption and . . . *yeah*," I say, pausing to face all of them. I drop my hands to my hips and take a calming breath. "We had a baby."

They're all facing me now. Six is looking at me like I'm suddenly not perfect anymore. "Daniel?" she whispers. "What the hell?"

She's mad at me. She's hurt that I would just blurt out the biggest secret she's ever had in her entire life.

I walk to her and place my hands on her shoulders. "I had to make the score even. We had to tell them. We know this really huge thing about them and unless they know *our* really huge thing, it wouldn't be even between us. Things would be weird."

I don't know if I'm making any sense to her.

"Six?" Sky whispers. "Is that true?"

Six pulls away from me and looks down. She nods, ashamed.

"Why didn't you tell me?"

Six looks back up at Sky. "Why didn't you tell me your name isn't even *Sky*?" Six says in defense.

Sky nods her head slowly, understanding that she can't really blame Six and Six can't really blame her. We're all even now. We stand quietly, each of us absorbing everything that's been revealed.

"Let's spit on it," I say. I hold my palm up and spit into my hand. "None of this will ever leave the room." I hold my hand out between the four of them and urge them to do the same.

"I'm not swapping spit with you," Sky says with a disgusted look on her face.

Six lifts her eyes to meet mine. "Me, neither," she says, crinkling up her nose.

I shake my head in confusion. "It's *spit*," I say. "You don't have a problem sticking your tongue in my mouth, but you won't touch a little spit with your hand?"

She winces. "That's different."

Holder steps forward and holds up his pinky. I laugh at him. "Really, Holder? You want us to *pinky* swear?"

He glares at me. "I'd like you to know there is nothing wrong with holding pinkies," he says defensively. "Now wipe the spit off your hand like a man and hold my damn pinky."

I can't believe I'm about to pinky swear. What are we, five?

I do what he asks and wipe my hand on my jeans, then we all step toward him. We wrap our pinkies together, and we all look each other in the eyes. No one says a word, because we don't have to. We all know that no matter what happens, everything we've learned about each other tonight will never leave this room.

Once we all release our pinkies, we step back and observe the moment silently. After several minutes of awkwardness, I turn to Six.

"Want to go make out at the park?"

She nods and expels a breath of relief. "Yep."

Thank God.

I turn to Holder and Sky. "We all still on for dinner at my house tomorrow night?"

Holder nods. "Sure. As long as you tell your dad he's not allowed to bring up anything embarrassing."

Has Holder not learned anything from watching me?

"He's my dad, Holder. If I tell him that, he'd take it as a dare."

Holder laughs. I step forward and pull him and Sky both in for a hug. I reach my arm behind me and grab Six, pulling her in with us. "Best friends forever," I tell them. "I love y'all so damn much."

They all groan and pull away from me. "Go make out with your girlfriend, Daniel," Holder says.

I wink at Six and push her toward the window.

I know it won't be tonight, but I'm still curious how long it'll be before she finally lets me pop her cork.

Nope. Still not sexy enough.

Smash her burger?

Oh God, no.

Plant my flower in her garden?

What the hell, Daniel?

Make love to her?

Yeah. That's it. That's the one.

• • •

The end.

Sneak Peek

Enjoy an excerpt from Colleen Hoover's new novel *Maybe Someday*, available now!

prologue

Sydney

I just punched a girl in the face. Not just *any* girl. My best friend. My roommate.

Well, as of five minutes ago, I guess I should call her my *ex*-roommate.

Her nose began bleeding almost immediately, and for a second, I felt bad for hitting her. But then I remembered what a lying, betraying whore she is, and it made me want to punch her again. I would have if Hunter hadn't prevented it by stepping between us.

So instead, I punched *him*. I didn't do any damage to him, unfortunately. Not like the damage I'd done to my hand.

Punching someone hurts a lot worse than I imagined it would. Not that I spend an excessive amount of time imagining how it would feel to punch people. Although I am having that urge again as I stare down at my phone at the incoming text from Ridge. He's another one I'd like to get even with. I know he technically has nothing to do with my current predicament, but he could have given me a heads-up a little sooner. Therefore, I'd like to punch him, too.

Ridge: Are you OK? Do u want to come up until the rain stops?

Of course I don't want to come up. My fist hurts enough as it is, and if I went up to Ridge's apartment, it would hurt a whole lot worse after I finished with him.

I turn around and look up at his balcony. He's leaning against his sliding-glass door; phone in hand, watching me. It's almost dark, but the lights from the courtyard illuminate his face. His dark eyes lock with mine and the way his mouth curls up into a soft, regretful smile makes it hard to remember why I'm even upset with him in the first place. He runs a free hand through the hair hanging loosely over his forehead, revealing even more of the worry in his expression. Or maybe that's a look of regret. As it should be.

I decide not to reply and flip him off instead. He shakes his head and shrugs his shoulders, as if to say, *I tried*, and then he goes back inside his apartment and slides his door shut.

I put the phone back in my pocket before it gets wet, and I look around at the courtyard of the apartment complex where I've lived for two whole months. When we first moved in, the hot Texas summer was swallowing up the last traces of spring, but this courtyard seemed to somehow still cling to life. Vibrant blue and purple hydrangeas lined the walkways leading up to the staircases and the fountain affixed in the center of the courtyard.

Now that summer has reached its most unattractive peak, the water in the fountain has long since evaporated. The hydrangeas are a sad, wilted reminder of the excitement I felt when Tori and I first moved in here. Looking at the courtyard now, defeated by the season, is an eerie parallel to how I feel at the moment. Defeated and sad.

I'm sitting on the edge of the now empty cement fountain, my elbows propped up on the two suitcases that contain most of my belongings, waiting for a cab to pick me up. I have no idea where it's going to take me, but I know I'd rather be anywhere except where I am right now. Which is, well, homeless.

I could call my parents, but that would give them ammunition to start firing all the *We told you so*'s at me.

We told you not to move so far away, Sydney.

We told you not to get serious with that guy.

We told you if you had chosen prelaw over music, we would have paid for it.

We told you to punch with your thumb on the outside *of your fist.*

Okay, maybe they never taught me the proper punching techniques, but if they're so right all the damn time, they *should* have.

I clench my fist, then spread out my fingers, then clench it again. My hand is surprisingly sore, and I'm pretty sure I should put ice on it. I feel sorry for guys. Punching sucks.

Know what else sucks? Rain. It always finds the most inappropriate time to fall, like right now, while I'm homeless.

The cab finally pulls up, and I stand and grab my suitcases. I roll them behind me as the cab driver gets out and pops open the trunk. Before I even hand him the first suitcase, my heart sinks as I suddenly realize that I don't even have my purse on me.

Shit.

I look around, back to where I was sitting on the suitcases, then feel around my body as if my purse will magically appear across my shoulder. But I know exactly where my purse is. I pulled it off my shoulder and dropped it to the floor right before I punched Tori in her overpriced Cameron Diaz nose.

I sigh. And I laugh. Of course I left my purse. My first day of being homeless would have been way too easy if I'd had a purse with me.

"I'm sorry," I say to the cab driver, who is now loading my second piece of luggage. "I changed my mind. I don't need a cab right now."

I know there's a hotel about a half-mile from here. If I can just work up the courage to go back inside and get my purse, I'll walk there and get a room until I figure out what to do. It's not as if I can get any wetter.

The driver takes the suitcases back out of the cab, sets them on the curb in front of me, and walks back to the driver's side without ever making eye contact. He just gets into his car and drives away, as if my canceling is a relief.

Do I look that pathetic?

I take my suitcases and walk back to where I was seated before I realized I was purseless. I glance up to my apartment and wonder what would happen if I went back there to get my wallet. I sort of left things in a mess when I walked out the door. I guess I'd rather be homeless in the rain than go back up there.

I take a seat on my luggage again and contemplate my situation. I could pay someone to go upstairs for me. But who? No one's outside, and who's to say Hunter or Tori would even give the person my purse?

This really sucks. I know I'm going to have to end up calling one of my friends, but right now, I'm too embarrassed to tell anyone how clueless I've been for the last two years. I've been completely blindsided.

I already hate being twenty-two, and I still have 364 more days to go.

It sucks so bad that I'm . . . *crying*?

Great. I'm crying now. I'm a purseless, crying, violent, homeless girl. And as much as I don't want to admit it, I think I might also be heartbroken.

Yep. Sobbing now. Pretty sure this must be what it feels like to have your heart broken.

"It's raining. Hurry up."

I glance up to see a girl hovering over me. She's holding an umbrella over her head and looking down at me with agitation while she hops from one foot to the other, waiting for me to do something. "I'm getting soaked. *Hurry.*"

Her voice is a little demanding, as if she's doing me some sort of favor and I'm being ungrateful. I arch an eyebrow as I look up at her, shielding the rain from my eyes with my hand. I don't know why she's complaining about getting wet, when there isn't much clothing to *get* wet. She's wearing next to nothing. I glance at her shirt, which is missing its entire bottom half, and realize she's in a Hooters outfit.

Could this day get any weirder? I'm sitting on almost everything I own in a torrential downpour, being bossed around by a bitchy Hooters waitress.

I'm still staring at her shirt when she grabs my hand and pulls me up in a huff. "Ridge said you would do this. I've got to get to work. Follow me, and I'll show you where the apartment is." She grabs one of my suitcases, pops the handle out, and shoves it at me. She takes the other and walks swiftly out of the courtyard. I follow her, for no other reason than the fact that she's taken one of my suitcases with her and I want it back.

She yells over her shoulder as she begins to ascend the stairwell. "I don't know how long you plan on staying, but I've only got one rule. Stay the hell out of my room."

She reaches an apartment and opens the door, never even looking back to see if I'm following her. Once I reach the top of the stairs, I pause outside the apartment and look down at the fern sitting unaffected by the heat in a planter outside the door. Its leaves are lush and green as if they're giving summer the middle finger with their refusal to succumb to the heat. I smile at the plant, somewhat proud of it. Then I frown with the realization that I'm envious of the resilience of a plant.

I shake my head, look away, then take a hesitant step inside the unfamiliar apartment. The layout is similar to my own apartment, only this one is a double split bedroom with four total bedrooms. My and Tori's apartment only had two bedrooms, but the living rooms are the same size.

The only other noticeable difference is that I don't see any lying, backstabbing, bloody-nosed whores standing in this one. Nor do I see any of Tori's dirty dishes or laundry lying around.

The girl sets my suitcase down beside the door, then steps aside and waits for me to . . . well, I don't know what she's waiting for me to do.

She rolls her eyes and grabs my arm, pulling me out of the door-way and further into the apartment. "What the hell is wrong with you? Do you even speak?" She begins to close the door behind her but pauses and turns around, wide-eyed. She holds her finger up in the air. "Wait," she says. "You're not . . ." She rolls her eyes and smacks herself in the forehead. "Oh, my God, you're deaf."

Huh? What the hell is wrong with this girl? I shake my head and start to answer her, but she interrupts me.

"God, Bridgette," she mumbles to herself. She rubs her hands down her face and groans, completely ignoring the fact that I'm shaking my head. "You're such an insensitive bitch sometimes."

Wow. This girl has some serious issues in the people-skills de-partment. She's sort of a bitch, even though she's making an effort not to be one. Now that she thinks I'm deaf. I don't even know how to respond. She shakes her head as if she's disappointed in herself, then looks straight at me.

"I . . . HAVE . . . TO . . . GO . . . TO . . . WORK . . . NOW!" she yells very loudly and painfully slowly. I grimace and step back, which should be a huge clue that I can hear her practically yelling, but she doesn't notice. She points to a door at the end of the hallway. "RIDGE . . . IS . . . IN . . . HIS . . . ROOM!"

Before I have a chance to tell her she can stop yelling, she leaves the apartment and closes the door behind her.

I have no idea what to think. Or what to do now. I'm standing, soaking wet, in the middle of an unfamiliar apartment, and the only person besides Hunter and Tori whom I feel like punching is now just a few feet away in another room. And speaking of Ridge, why the hell did he send his psycho Hooters girlfriend to get me? I take out my phone and have begun to text him when his bedroom door opens.

He walks out into the hallway with an armful of blankets and a pillow. As soon as he makes eye contact with me, I gasp. I hope it's not a noticeable gasp. It's just that I've never actually seen him up close before, and he's even better looking from just a few feet away than he is from across an apartment courtyard.

I don't think I've ever seen eyes that can actually speak. I'm not sure what I mean by that. It just seems as if he could shoot me the tiniest glance with those dark eyes of his, and I'd know exactly what they needed me to do. They're piercing and intense and—oh, my God, I'm staring.

The corner of his mouth tilts up in a knowing smile as he passes me and heads straight for the couch.

Despite his appealing and slightly innocent-looking face, I want to yell at him for being so deceitful. He shouldn't have waited more than two weeks to tell me. I would have had a chance to plan all this out a little better. I don't understand how we could have had two weeks' worth of conversations without his feeling the need to tell me that my boyfriend and my best friend were screwing.

Ridge throws the blankets and the pillow onto the couch.

"I'm not staying here, Ridge," I say, attempting to stop him from wasting time with his hospitality. I know he feels bad for me, but I hardly know him, and I'd feel a lot more comfortable in a hotel room than sleeping on a strange couch.

Then again, hotel rooms require money.

Something I don't have on me at the moment.

Something that's inside my purse, across the courtyard, in an apartment with the only two people in the world I don't want to see right now.

Maybe a couch isn't such a bad idea after all.

He gets the couch made up and turns around, dropping his eyes to my soaking-wet clothes. I look down at the puddle of water I'm creating in the middle of his floor.

"Oh, sorry," I mutter. My hair is matted to my face; my shirt is now a see-through pathetic excuse for a barrier between the outside world and my very pink, very noticeable bra. "Where's your bathroom?"

He nods his head toward the bathroom door.

I turn around, unzip a suitcase, and begin to rummage through it while Ridge walks back into his bedroom. I'm glad he doesn't ask me questions about what happened after our conversation earlier. I'm not in the mood to talk about it.

I select a pair of yoga pants and a tank top, then grab my bag of toiletries and head to the bathroom. It disturbs me that everything about this apartment reminds me of my own, with just a few subtle differences. This is the same bathroom with the Jack-and-Jill doors on the left and right, leading to the two bedrooms that adjoin it. One is Ridge's, obviously. I'm curious about who the other bedroom belongs to but not curious enough to open it. The Hooters girl's one rule was to stay the hell out of her room, and she doesn't seem like the type to kid around.

I shut the door that leads to the living room and lock it, then check the locks on both doors to the bedrooms to make sure no one can walk in. I have no idea if anyone lives in this apartment other than Ridge and the Hooters girl, but I don't want to chance it.

I pull off my sopping clothes and throw them into the sink to avoid soaking the floor. I turn on the shower and wait until the water gets warm, then step in. I stand under the stream of water and close my eyes, thankful that I'm not still sitting outside in the rain. At the same time, I'm not really happy to be where I am, either.

I never expected my twenty-second birthday to end with me showering in a strange apartment and sleeping on a couch that belongs to a guy I've barely known for two weeks, all at the hands of the two people I cared about and trusted the most.

1.

Sydney

I slide open my balcony door and step outside, thankful that the sun has already dipped behind the building next door, cooling the air to what could pass as a perfect fall temperature. Almost on cue, the sound of his guitar floats across the courtyard as I take a seat and lean back into the patio lounger. I tell Tori I come out here to get homework done, because I don't want to admit that the guitar is the only reason I'm outside every night at eight, like clockwork.

For weeks now, the guy in the apartment across the courtyard has sat on his balcony and played for at least an hour. Every night, I sit outside and listen.

I've noticed a few other neighbors come out to their balconies when he's playing, but no one is as loyal as I am. I don't understand how someone could hear these songs and not crave them day after day. Then again, music has always been a passion of mine, so maybe I'm just a little more infatuated with his sound than other people are. I've played the piano for as long as I can remember, and although I've never shared it with anyone, I love writing music. I even switched my major to music education two years ago. My plan is to be an elementary music teacher, although if my father had his way, I'd still be prelaw.

"A life of mediocrity is a waste of a life," he said when I informed him that I was changing my major.

A life of mediocrity. I find that more amusing than insulting, since he seems to be the most dissatisfied person I've ever known. And he's a lawyer. Go figure.

One of the familiar songs ends and the guy with the guitar begins to play something he's never played before. I've grown accustomed to his unofficial playlist since he seems to practice the same songs in the same order night after night. However, I've never heard him play this particular song before. The way he's repeating the same chords makes me think he's creating the song right here on the spot. I like that I'm witnessing this, especially since after only a few chords, it's already my new favorite. All his songs sound like originals. I wonder if he performs them locally or if he just writes them for fun.

I lean forward in the chair, rest my arms on the edge of the balcony, and watch him. His balcony is directly across the courtyard, far enough away that I don't feel weird when I watch him but close enough that I make sure I'm never watching him when Hunter's around. I don't think Hunter would like the fact that I've developed a tiny crush on this guy's talent.

I can't deny it, though. Anyone who watches how passionately this guy plays would crush on his talent. The way he keeps his eyes closed the entire time, focusing intently on every stroke against every guitar string. I like it best when he sits cross-legged with the guitar upright between his legs. He pulls it against his chest and plays it like a stand-up bass, keeping his eyes closed the whole time. It's so mesmerizing to watch him that sometimes I catch myself holding my breath, and I don't even realize I'm doing it until I'm gasping for air.

It also doesn't help that he's cute. At least, he seems cute from here. His light brown hair is unruly and moves with him, falling across his forehead every time he looks down at his guitar. He's too far away to distinguish eye color or distinct features, but the details don't matter when coupled with the passion he has for his music. There's a confidence to him that I find compelling. I've always admired musicians who are able to tune out everyone and everything around them and pour all of their focus into their music. To be able to shut the world off and allow yourself to be completely swept away is something I've always wanted the confidence to do, but I just don't have it.

This guy has it. He's confident and talented. I've always been a sucker for musicians, but more in a fantasy way. They're a different breed. A breed that rarely makes for good boyfriends.

He glances at me as if he can hear my thoughts, and then a slow grin appears across his face. He never once pauses the song while he continues to watch me. The eye contact makes me blush, so I drop my arms and pull my notebook back onto my lap and look down at it. I hate that he just caught me staring so hard. Not that I was doing anything wrong; it just feels odd for him to know I was watching him. I glance up again, and he's still watching me, but he's not smiling anymore. The way he's staring causes my heart to speed up, so I look away and focus on my notebook.

Way to be a creeper, Sydney.

"There's my girl," a comforting voice says from behind me. I lean my head back and tilt my eyes upward to watch Hunter as he makes his way onto the balcony. I try to hide the fact that I'm shocked to see him, because I'm pretty sure I was supposed to remember he was coming.

On the off chance that Guitar Boy is still watching, I make it a point to seem really into Hunter's hello kiss so that maybe I'll seem less like a creepy stalker and more like someone just casually relaxing on her balcony. I run my hand up Hunter's neck as he leans over the back of my chair and kisses me upside down.

"Scoot up," Hunter says, pushing on my shoulders. I do what he asks and slide forward in the seat as he lifts his leg over the chair and slips in behind me. He pulls my back against his chest and wraps his arms around me.

My eyes betray me when the sound of the guitar stops abruptly, and I glance across the courtyard once more. Guitar Boy is eyeing us hard as he stands, then goes back inside his apartment. His expression is odd. Almost angry.

"How was school?" Hunter asks.

"Too boring to talk about. What about you? How was work?"

"Interesting," he says, brushing my hair away from my neck with his hand. He presses his lips to my neck and kisses his way down my collarbone.

"What was so interesting?"

He tightens his hold on me, then rests his chin on my shoulder and pulls me back in the chair with him. "The oddest thing happened at lunch," he says. "I was with one of the guys at this Italian restaurant. We were eating out on the patio, and I had just asked the waiter what he recommended for dessert, when a police car rounded the corner. They stopped right in front of the restaurant, and two officers jumped out with their guns drawn. They began barking orders toward us when our waiter mumbled, 'Shit.' He slowly raised his hands, and the police jumped the barrier to the patio, rushed toward him, threw him to the ground, and cuffed him right at our feet. After they read him his rights, they pulled him to his feet and escorted him toward the cop car. The waiter glanced back at me and yelled, 'The tiramisu is really good!' Then they put him in the car and drove away."

I tilt my head back and look up at him. "Seriously? That really happened?"

He nods, laughing. "I swear, Syd. It was crazy."

"Well? Did you try the tiramisu?"

"Hell, yeah, we did. It was the best tiramisu I've ever had." He kisses me on the cheek and pushes me forward. "Speaking of food, I'm starving." He stands up and holds out his hand to me. "Did you cook tonight?"

I take his hand and let him pull me up. "We just had salad, but I can make you one."

Once we're inside, Hunter takes a seat on the couch next to Tori. She's got a textbook spread open across her lap as she halfheartedly focuses on both homework and TV at the same time. I take out the containers from the fridge and make his salad. I feel a little guilty that I forgot tonight was one of the nights he said he was coming. I usually have something cooked when I know he'll be here.

We've been dating for almost two years now. I met him during my sophomore year in college, when he was a senior. He and Tori had been friends for years. After she moved into my dorm and we became friends, she insisted I meet him. She said we'd hit it off, and she was right. We made it official after only two dates, and things have been wonderful since.

Of course, we have our ups and downs, especially since he moved more than an hour away. When he landed the job in the accounting firm last semester, he suggested I move with him. I told him no, that I really wanted to finish my undergrad before taking such a huge step. In all honesty, I'm just scared.

The thought of moving in with him seems so final, as if I would be sealing my fate. I know that once we take that step, the next step is marriage, and then I'd be looking at never having the chance to live alone. I've always had a roommate, and until I can afford my own place, I'll be sharing an apartment with Tori. I haven't told Hunter yet, but I really want to live alone for a year. It's something I promised myself I would do before I got married. I don't even turn twenty-two for a couple of weeks, so it's not as if I'm in any hurry.

I take Hunter's food to him in the living room.

"Why do you watch this?" he says to Tori. "All these women do is talk shit about each other and flip tables."

"That's exactly why I watch it," Tori says, without taking her eyes off the TV.

Hunter winks at me and takes his food, then props his feet up on the coffee table. "Thanks, babe." He turns toward the TV and begins eating. "Can you grab me a beer?"

I nod and walk back into the kitchen. I open the refrigerator door and look on the shelf where he always keeps his extra beer. I realize as I'm staring at "his" shelf that this is probably how it begins. First, he has a shelf in the refrigerator. Then he'll have a toothbrush in the bathroom, a drawer in my dresser, and eventually, his stuff will infiltrate mine in so many ways it'll be impossible for me ever to be on my own.

I run my hands up my arms, rubbing away the sudden onset of discomfort washing over me. I feel as if I'm watching my future play out in front of me. I'm not so sure I like what I'm imagining.

Am I ready for this?

Am I ready for this guy to be the guy I bring dinner to every night when he gets home from work?

Am I ready to fall into this comfortable life with him? One where I teach all day and he does people's taxes, and then we come home and I cook dinner and I "grab him beers" while he props his feet up and calls me *babe*, and then we go to our bed and make love at approximately nine P.M. so we won't be tired the next day, in order to wake up and get dressed and go to work and do it all over again?

"Earth to Sydney," Hunter says. I hear him snap his fingers twice. "Beer? Please, babe?"

I quickly grab his beer, give it to him, then head straight to my bathroom. I turn the water on in the shower, but I don't get in. Instead, I lock the door and sink to the floor.

We have a good relationship. He's good to me, and I know he loves me. I just don't understand why every time I think about a future with him, it's not an exciting thought.

Ridge

Maggie leans forward and kisses my forehead. "I need to go."

I'm on my back with my head and shoulders partially propped against my headboard. She's straddling my lap and looking down at me regretfully. I hate that we live so far apart now, but it makes the time we do spend together a lot more meaningful. I take her hands so she'll shut up, and I pull her to me, hoping to persuade her not to leave just yet.

She laughs and shakes her head. She kisses me, but only briefly, and then she pulls away again. She slides off my lap, but I don't let her make it very far before I lunge forward and pin her to the mattress. I point to her chest.

"You"—I lean in and kiss the tip of her nose—"need to stay one more night."

"I can't. I have class."

I grab her wrists and pin her arms above her head, then press my lips to hers. I know she won't stay another night. She's never missed a day of class in her life, unless she was too sick to move. I sort of wish she was feeling a little sick right now, so I could make her stay in bed with me.

I slide my hands from her wrists, delicately up her arms until I'm cupping her face. Then I give her one final kiss before I reluctantly pull away from her. "Go. And be careful. Let me know when you make it home."

She nods and pushes herself off the bed. She reaches across me and grabs her shirt, then pulls it on over her head. I watch her as she walks around the room and gathers the clothes I pulled off her in a hurry.

After five years of dating, most couples would have moved in together by now. However, most peoples' other halves aren't Maggie. She's so fiercely independent it's almost intimidating. But it's understandable, considering how her life has gone. She's been caring for her grandfather since I met her. Before that, she spent the majority of her teenage years helping him care for her grandmother, who died when Maggie was sixteen. Now that her grandfather is in a nursing home, she finally has a chance to live alone while finishing school, and as much as I want her here with me, I also know how important this internship is for her. So for the next year, I'll suck it up while she's in San Antonio and I'm here in Austin. I'll be damned if I ever move out of Austin, especially for San Antonio.

Unless she asked, of course.

"Tell your brother I said good luck." She's standing in my bedroom doorway, poised to leave. "And you need to quit beating yourself up, Ridge. Musicians have blocks, just like writers do. You'll find your muse again. I love you."

"I love you, too."

She smiles and backs out of my bedroom. I groan, knowing she's trying to be positive with the whole writer's block thing, but I can't stop stressing about it. I don't know if it's because Brennan has so much riding on these songs now or if it's because I'm completely tapped out, but the words just aren't coming. Without lyrics I'm confident in, it's hard to feel good about the actual musical aspect of writing.

My phone vibrates. It's a text from Brennan, which only makes me feel worse about the fact that I'm stuck.

Brennan: It's been weeks. Please tell me you have something.

Me: Working on it. How's the tour?

Brennan: Good, but remind me not to allow Warren to schedule this many gigs on the next leg.

Me: Gigs are what gets your name out there.

Brennan: OUR name. I'm not telling you again to stop acting like you aren't half of this.

Me: I won't be half if I can't work through this damn block.

Brennan: Maybe you should get out more. Cause some unnecessary drama in your life. Break up with Maggie for the sake of art. She'll understand. Heartache helps with lyrical inspiration. Don't you ever listen to country?

Me: Good idea. I'll tell Maggie you suggested that.

Brennan: Nothing I say or do could ever make Maggie hate me. Give her a kiss for me, and get to writing. Our careers are resting squarely on your shoulders.

Me: Asshole.

Brennan: Ah! Is that anger I detect in your text? Use it. Go write an angry song about how much you hate your little brother, then send it to me. ;)

Me: Yeah. I'll give it to you after you finally get your shit out of your old bedroom. Bridgette's sister might move in next month.

Brennan: Have you ever met Brandi?

Me: No. Do I want to?

Brennan: Only if you want to live with two Bridgettes.

Me: Oh, shit.

Brennan: Exactly. TTYL.

I close out the text to Brennan and open up a text to Warren.

Me: We're good to go on the roommate search. Brennan says hell no to Brandi. I'll let you break the news to Bridgette, since you two get along so well.

Warren: Well, motherfucker.

I laugh and hop off the bed, then head to the patio with my guitar. It's almost eight, and I know she'll be on her balcony. I don't know how weird my actions are about to seem to her, but all I can do is try. I've got nothing to lose.

About the Author

Colleen Hoover is the #1 *New York Times* bestselling author of *Slammed*, *Point of Retreat*, *Hopeless*, *This Girl*, and *Losing Hope*. Colleen lives in Texas with her husband and their three boys. Please visit her Facebook page at www.facebook.com/authorcolleenhoover and her website at ColleenHoover.com.

Don't miss the highly anticipated sequel to the
"riveting" (*Kirkus Reviews,* starred review)
#1 *New York Times* bestselling novel

IT ENDS WITH US

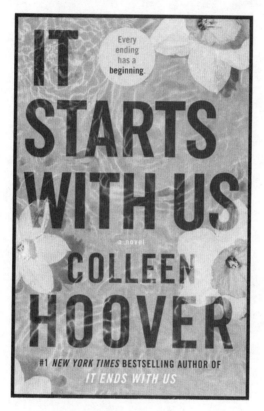

Every
ending
has a
beginning.

IT
STARTS
WITH US

a novel

COLLEEN
HOOVER

#1 *NEW YORK TIMES* BESTSELLING AUTHOR OF
IT ENDS WITH US

Available **October 2022** wherever books are sold or
at SimonandSchuster.com

ATRIA
BOOKS